MORNING
IS ALWAYS
NIGH

MORNING

IS ALWAYS

NIGH

A Colorado Boyhood

A Novel by John Wickersham

Illustrations by Jamie Wickersham

WPP

WOODEN PANTS PUBLISHING

Printed in the United States of America
First Printing, 2016
Wooden Pants Publishing

Book design by: Jennifer Schafer
Edited by: Nancy L. Reed

ISBN-13: 978-0-9973535-7-0
ISBN-10: 0-9973535-7-0

DEDICATION

For Catherine L. and Sumner R. Wickersham,
who loved their children beyond measure

CONTENTS

ILLUSTRATIONS

ACKNOWLEDGEMENTS

For more than fifty years, I have told stories to my students, spoonfuls of sugar to help the medicine of philosophy go down. Over the years, many have suggested that I write up these stories. When I had gathered several together, I showed them to Janet Edwards, a colleague and a fine writer, asking for her opinion. She suggested how I might fashion this little gaggle of stories into a larger conception, the reflection of a man upon his boyhood. I am deeply appreciative.

My niece, Katie Hall has been my editor and best critic from the beginning. I also want to thank my publisher, Rich Keller, his editor, Nan Reed, and his designer, Jennifer Schafer. To them I owe much. Chris Patton, a former student now an interactive designer, did the graphics. Bob Tschopp, another former student and now an IT professional, rescued me continually from the technical muddles into which I regularly got myself while writing the manuscript.

My son, Jamie, collaborated with me, providing the drawings that make the book not just a book, but a physically beautiful thing. Read the book; if it has any distinction, it is largely due to Jamie's art. Finally, I want to thank my wife, Barbara, friend and fellow-traveler for over fifty years, for reasons that both she and I understand.

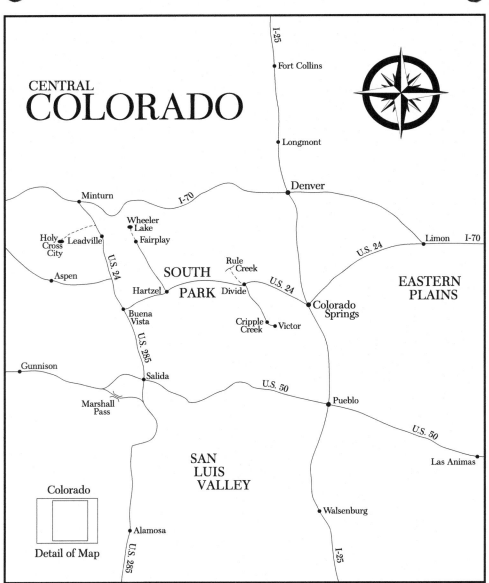

CENTRAL
COLORADO

I-25

Fort Collins

Longmont

Denver

Minturn   I-70

Wheeler
Lake
Holy   Fairplay
Cross Leadville
City
Aspen   U.S. 24   SOUTH

Rule
Creek
Hartzel   PARK   Divide   U.S. 24

Buena   Colorado
Vista   Springs

Cripple   Victor
Creek

Gunnison   U.S. 285

Salida

Marshall
Pass   U.S. 50   Pueblo

Limon   I-70

EASTERN
PLAINS

U.S. 24

SAN
LUIS
VALLEY

U.S. 50

Las Animas

Colorado

Detail of Map

Walsenburg

Alamosa

U.S. 285

I-25

PROLOGUE

Molly rocked back and forth in the wooden rocker, flush with nostalgia. This chair had been in the family room when she was a child. She'd loved rocking slowly and reading there in the evening just before she went to bed. Now it adorned her dad's office at the university where the late afternoon sunlight fell softly on these two, the daughter and her father whom she resembled strongly.

Molly had come to St. Louis over Christmas, having traveled with her husband and two girls from their Colorado home to spend a week with her parents, Helen and Dan Gray. The Gray children gathered annually at their parents' St. Louis home for a maddening, wonderful week they'd come to call with affection "family stress encounter." This evening, the whole family was going out for supper, so she stopped by to pick her father up. She purposely came early in order to visit with him for a little while in the quiet of his office. She rarely found the opportunity to speak with him alone.

"So, what's the story, Dad?" Molly began.

She posed her question as a rhetorical joke, but her father, Dan, picked up on it.

"Funny you should ask. I've been thinking about stories. Now, after all these years, it's hard for me to tell the difference between my stories and my life. They've run together over time."

"As a little girl, I loved listening to your stories. I guess I've heard most of them a hundred times, but I never tire of them. They always made me feel bigger and older, and it pleased me that I played a role in them."

"Stories are strangely powerful," he responded. "I'm notorious here for salting my courses with them. It's how I gain the affection and trust of my students. Everyone has a story; everyone loves a story."

"I've always thought this was a big reason for Plato's immense influence down through the centuries. His *Dialogues* are full of wonderful stories," Molly replied. She had a graduate education in philosophy and classics, and in her view, Plato reigned as the greatest of the lovers of wisdom.

"Think about 'The Allegory of the Cave,' or, 'The Myth of Er.' Those two alone put Plato in the first rank of storytellers. What is it about stories, Dad, that charms us so?"

"I think it's the way they connect us to one another, to all humankind for that matter. A good story invites the listener to step into an imaginary world, a world of beautiful things or scary things or endearing things. The listener almost always takes away a lesson."

Dan stood up and retrieved a small wooden tablet from a shelf high in his bookcase. It was honey brown and glowed with the luster of much handled old wood. On this tablet faint handwriting described how his great-grandfather, Emanuel Fleisher, once evaded the attack of a bull buffalo by climbing into a box elder tree from which this chip came. That incident occurred in 1878, when Emanuel lived with his wife and children on a homestead in north central Kansas.

Dan looked at the wood intently for a moment and then read it aloud, pausing from time to time over the faded text.

"That's such a great story. In my mind's eye, I can watch the whole thing unfold like an old movie," Molly said. "Through a wonderful alchemy, he reaches out and touches me."

"Such stories help us hold on to our past," Dan continued, "even though those times have slipped into the river of the years. Now, in the autumn of my life, I find myself continually thinking of my family. Your faces all appear before me when I lie in bed reciting my night prayers. It makes me mindful of how the thread of my life is being spun out. The image that comes to mind is Bryant's 'innumerable caravan' of man.

"You know, Sweetheart, the legacy of my parents and grandparents is a tapestry woven of love and light. My worry is that it will fade away over time, like the story on the tablet, and cease to *be* for me and to *mean* for me. I worry that for my siblings and our sizable brood of children and grandchildren, this will eventually be a lost world."

"Well, Dad, why don't you do something about it? Write the stories down. It would be a great gift to us all."

"But, there are simply too many," he objected.

"Then, why don't you isolate a period of time in your life you remember as particularly rich and interesting," Molly suggested. "Tell us those stories. Help us to cherish them."

"I guess I could do that. I remember especially one year, a kind of *annus mirabilis,* a remarkable time when I was twelve years old. There were two summers bookending an autumn, winter, and spring, a splendid year for the whole family. As Browning put it, God was in His heaven, and all was right with the world. For me personally, that time, from the spring of 1956 until the fall of 1957, proved essential. During that year, I first dimly grasped the idea that we are wayfarers. I began to see my life as a journey and to see myself searching for a path. Of course, being only twelve, I didn't grasp this idea in an adult way."

"That would be perfect, Dad. When will you start? You've told these stories many times, but writing them down will be altogether different. It might be an emotional roller coaster, actually sorting them out and reliving them intensely and vividly. Write them from the point of view of a twelve-year-old boy. Help us see what you saw and feel what you felt."

"I don't know, Sweetheart; we'll have to see."

A few days later, Helen and Dan saw their out-of-town kids off to their homes in Colorado.

"It will be so lonely around here with the kids gone," Helen said, a trace of sadness in her voice.

"That's true," Dan responded. "Parting is sorrowful, and there's nothing sweet about it."

Dan brooded. When Molly had kissed him good bye, she'd whispered sternly, "Write the stories, Dad!" Her tone told all; she didn't think he would write about his Colorado boyhood.

He excused himself. "Honey, I'm going upstairs to do some work on the computer."

Sitting in front of it, he stared at the blank white screen. His thoughts drifted back to the old days in Colorado Springs. He imagined the Front Range of the mountains. Slowly, he began to type:

It was time once more for the yearly miracle. Someday soon, billowing clouds would march along the Rampart Range ...

ONE

DANNY GRAY RESCUES A TROUT

And when white moths were on the wing,
And moth-like stars were flickering out,
I dropped the berry in a stream
And caught a little silver trout.
— William B. Yeats —

It was time once more for the yearly miracle. Someday soon, billowing clouds would march along the Rampart Range, sending a warm wind sliding down the mountain slopes, bringing a message to the greening prairie from the sun and the deep sky. *Rejoice*, the wind would whisper, *summer is here.*

Danny Gray grew up on this prairie and in these mountains. He lived with his mom and dad, and his sister and brother in a house in the foothills of the Colorado Rockies. At the age of twelve, Danny was all boy – impish, curious, imaginative, yet tenderhearted. His blue-green eyes were set off by his auburn hair.

Every morning, when Danny walked out the front door, the sight of Pikes Peak amazed him with its skirt of lesser mountains spreading north and south to both horizons. Only dimly did he appreciate his privilege as one of the darlings of destiny, born into a loving family and living in a house near these beautiful mountains. He didn't trouble himself about the reasons for this. It didn't matter; his world seemed plain wonderful, whatever the reasons.

His sister, Mary, was blue-eyed and blond and two years older, and in her own mind, superior to him in every way. However, all things considered, they were good friends and companions.

Danny's older brother, John, was a kind of hero to him. Danny admired the ease and grace with which John did nearly everything.

Danny's father, Russell, grew up on a farm near Palisade on Colorado's Western Slope. Like most farm boys, Russell hunted and fished avidly, at home in the outdoors and happiest in the mountains. He was a wise, generous man with a ready smile.

Louise, Danny's mother, was the daughter of a locomotive engineer on the Denver and Rio Grande Railroad. Her father, an Irish immigrant, came to Colorado seeking a new life. Her red hair set off her light blue eyes, which were beautiful even when stern with Danny. And that was often.

———◆———

One April morning in 1956, looking at the mountains from his front porch, Danny felt something new, the dawning of thoughts and hopes about the future, things he'd never felt before. For the first time, he began to see his life as a story and that he stood at the first chapter. The rest had yet to be written.

Long ago, Aristotle theorized the world is driven by a universal longing, that everything has a destiny to fulfill, a path determined by its inner nature. This striving of natural things toward a fullness of being he called flourishing.

Of course, Danny knew nothing of Aristotle, and he'd never before thought of his life this way. The dawning sense of direction was new to him, an altogether thrilling idea, although he didn't fully understand it. He was becoming aware of moving toward something. This would be a fine summer, the best summer yet.

Later that day, while his mother prepared supper, Danny stood beside her at the kitchen counter.

"Mom, a neat thing happened today."

"And what was that?" she asked.

"Down in the woods, I saw a tree limb pretty far above my head.

Out of nowhere I got an idea. I just decided to jump up and grab it. I didn't think I could, but I did! I pulled myself up and got on the limb. I felt really strong. It seemed like a thing Johnny could do. I loved it!"

She smiled. "Ah, Danny, I know what you're feeling, and it's good. You're growing up."

The Gray home stood at the end of a gravel road. The road ran along the top of a low ridge, and scrub oak woods fell away from their backyard into a valley. At the end of the valley nestled a small lake fed by several springs in the nearby hills. One such spring rose in the woods only a hundred yards below the house. It was a tiny thing seeping from under a sandstone slab. The water flowed clear and cold, the beginning of a creek that fed the lake. Right where the spring emerged there was a pool the size of a bathtub edged with grass and wild flowers. In the dark center, the water reached a depth of about eight inches. The spring undercut the rock slab making a kind of hidden pocket.

On many occasions, the Gray kids drank the cold, delicious water from this spring. The spring and the little copse around it were one of those treasured secret places. Mary liked to sit on the grass and write in her poetry notebook. By now, she'd written a half-dozen she called her "spring poems."

For his part, Danny had taught himself how to whittle with his Barlow knife. On the grass beside the spring, he once whittled a boat out of a stick, turned by imagination into a Viking longship, and launched it onto the dark, tormented sea of the spring pool.

As for John, he liked to read beside the spring. He'd taken three years of Latin at St. Mary's, and this year, the class had studied Horace's *Odes*. His favorite of these old poems was "The Spring of Bandusia" which Horace dedicated to a spring on his farm in the Sabine Hills south of Rome. In the last line, Horace remarked about its "talkative waters," as if he were writing especially for the kids and their secret spring. John memorized most of the ode so he could enjoy it whenever he wanted.

One afternoon when Mary, Danny, and he were lounging on the grass beside the spring, John began reciting,

> "O fons bandusiae, splendidior vitro,
> dulci digno mero non sine floribus…
> fies nobilium tu quoque fontium
> me dicente cavis impositam ilicem
> saxis unde loquaces lymphae desiliunt tuae."

"What does it mean, Johnny," Danny asked.
"Well, let me see," he began,

> "O spring of Bandusia, more brilliant than glass,
> worthy of sweet wine and not without flowers…
> indeed, you will become an illustrious spring
> once I sing about the oak beside the grotto
> whence flow your talkative waters."

John's recitation wasn't an unusual event. His mother's Irish family came from singers and poets. She'd been taught by the Jesuits in high school in east Denver where she'd put in four arduous years studying Latin, English literature, and American literature. Russell's mother, Ruth, had earned a college degree as a music teacher. She was widowed early in her marriage. As a result, Russell's grandfather, Emanuel, who was a minister in the German Synod of the Methodist Church, served as his father. As a child, Russell studied the scriptures in German with his grandpa. Later, he attended the University of Colorado for a year before he withdrew because of the Great Depression. They didn't have an Ivy League pedigree, but both Louise and Russell were learned in the old fashioned way, avid readers, and lovers of poetry.

Danny's dad owned the Green Pine Restaurant on Pikes Peak Avenue in downtown Colorado Springs. Danny's grandma, Ruth, owned a bakery and tea room, Ruth's Kitchen, on Tejon Street. Despite the fact that the two establishments were somewhat different, Russell and his mom were both in the restaurant business and were friendly competitors.

For Danny, Mary, and John, the restaurants were a world of interesting people and good food. All three worked in the summer washing dishes, helping the cooks, and minding the storerooms. In the winter, when the days were pale and cold, Danny often stopped by the Green Pine on his way home from school to have a plate of French fries smothered in chili. The chef, Luis Valdez, always seemed to have a story to tell him in Spanish. Luis had called him "little brother" since Danny's early childhood.

"¿*Cómo estás, hermanito*?" Luis would always begin. He would then launch into a colorful tale from his boyhood in Alamosa. Luis coached Danny along with the meanings of words until he could understand the story.

Luis, a complex man, had struggled with his personal demons for many years. Russell was patient with him, and the bond between the two ran genuine and deep. As a result, Luis was always solicitous of the Gray kids, particularly of Danny. Without actually trying, Danny learned to speak some Spanish as a result of Luis's lessons.

Spanish people emigrated into what is now Colorado in the eighteenth century. Several towns in the San Luis Valley dated from that era. Thus, Danny not only spoke a little Spanish with Luis, but he could also charlar with several of his classmates. He enjoyed learning Spanish, but he also liked the cachet it lent him in his continuous efforts to maintain himself against his siblings. Whenever John or Mary asserted their superiority to him, a Spanish quip would generally put an end to the matter, because his brother and sister would usually be at a loss for a response.

One day in the late spring of 1956, when Danny entered the Green Pine kitchen, an unusual thing happened. A man named Fred Wilson stood in the center of a group of the kitchen crew showing them

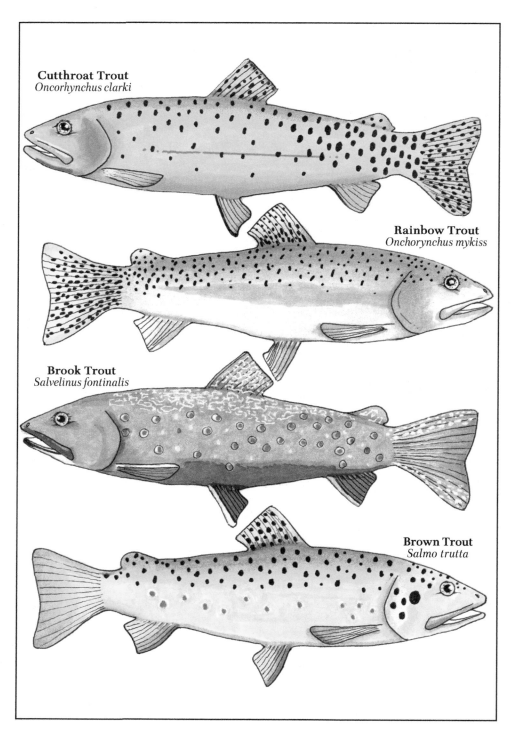

Cutthroat Trout
Oncorhynchus clarki

Rainbow Trout
Onchorynchus mykiss

Brook Trout
Salvelinus fontinalis

Brown Trout
Salmo trutta

Trout of Colorado

something. Danny joined them to see what he held. In a small galvanized pail half-full of water swam a beautiful rainbow trout. Mr. Wilson owned a trout farm up in the mountains on West Creek, north of Divide. He raised trout and sold them to restaurants and markets. On this occasion, he brought in a live rainbow trout to show Luis and the other cooks. Most of them had only seen these fish when they prepared them for cooking. The rainbow was frantic, splashing around in the pail, its dorsal stripe flashing rose-vermillion, banging its head against the sides.

"What are you going to do with it, Mr. Wilson?" Danny asked.

"Well, Danny, it will join its friends in the cooler and be someone's supper tonight."

"Please don't do that. Let me keep it and take it home."

"Well, Danny, that's up to your dad, although I don't think a trout will make much of a pet. You mustn't take it to bed with you!" he said, winking at Luis.

This amiable joke typified the way the kitchen crew treated the Gray kids whom they considered part of the restaurant family. Pricey Wills, who prepared all the soups, gravies, and sauces, used to carry Danny, when a toddler, around the kitchen in a bushel basket. She reminded him of this whenever he came into the kitchen.

When they all laughed at Fred Wilson's little joke, Danny laughed with them.

Riding home with his dad after work, the pail cradled carefully on his lap, Danny was happy. He explained to his dad what he wanted to do. The spring pool would be a perfect place for his trout. Only he, John, and Mary knew about the spring, so his new friend would be safe.

Russell smiled as Danny rattled on about his plans for Fred the Trout. However, he suspected the fish was doomed much like the baby rabbits, the abandoned fledgling birds, and all the creatures his kids found over the years. He knew wild things rarely do well in the company of people. Nevertheless, he told Danny to handle the trout carefully when he released him into the spring pool; perhaps Fred would make it after all.

Danny was no stranger to fish. From his early childhood, he'd been initiated by his dad into the outdoor life and the lore of woodsmen. On many an afternoon, from age five on, he waited on the front porch for his father to come home so they could hike down to the lake and fly fish.

When the Plymouth station wagon pulled into the driveway, Danny climbed out carefully, taking care not to startle Fred. He placed the pail in the shade of the open garage and yelled into the house for John and Mary to come and see his treasure. John came out quickly, curious about Danny's surprise. Mary followed John, trying not to seem curious, certain that nothing Danny thought to be important could actually be so. However, both she and John were amazed to see the fish swimming in tight circles in the bottom of the pail.

"Come on!" gushed Danny excitedly. "Let's put Fred in the spring."

The three rambled down the faint path toward the woods. At one point the path crossed an unshaded patch of red granite gravel. Scattered across this miniature desert were some yucca and prickly pear cacti. The kids were always watchful when they crossed the sunlit glade, a favorite spot for rattlesnakes to warm themselves. One late spring day the year before, Danny found himself among four big prairie rattlesnakes warming themselves in the sun. The largest of them easily reached five feet.

"Watch out for the snakes," Danny cautioned. "There's one big boy that hangs around under that patch of yucca. I've seen him a couple of times, and he kind of knows me. He won't do anything if we don't bother him."

John carried the heavy pail; Danny and Mary followed. Russell had warned them not to touch the fish if at all possible. Trout, he said, are covered with a slick film that protects them from diseases. The film could be rubbed off if they handled Fred carelessly. Hence, it would be best to pour the contents of the pail – fish, water, and all – gently into the spring pool.

As soon as Fred slid out of the pail, he immediately darted under the rock slab and out of sight. The three stepped back several feet from the pool and sat in the shade of a scrub oak. They neither moved nor spoke. In several minutes, Fred peeked out from his hideout and cautiously swam into the pool. A water skipper pranced blithely over the surface of the spring pool. In an instant, Fred shot up out of the water, grabbed the skipper, and dove back in. The three laughed with delight.

This trout affair typified the Gray family. John, Mary, and Danny attended the parish school, but their parents didn't leave the development of their religious sensibility to the nuns and the catechism. They often discussed religion at the supper table, and their discussions weren't shallow and doctrinaire. Long before deep ecology became fashionable, they talked about the sacramental character of the world and the holiness of natural things. This was an important part of the legacy from Louise and Russell to their children.

Russell also gave them his inherited love for books and words, and he frequently commented on the use of language in family conversations. Louise passed along her Irish heritage. In her family, being loyal to the past, being steadfast and resolute, were of utmost importance. Her family typified those Irish who suffered under the long and brutal British occupation of their native land. As a result, quite unconsciously, she made her kids strong. And so, the matter of Fred the Trout wasn't what it might seem to an outsider. The whole family took interest, and they hoped there would be a happy outcome from putting the fish in the spring pool.

The kids' walk from the spring back to the house was exceptionally beautiful. Yellow afternoon light filtered through the scrub oak, dancing on them and dappling the trail. When the three reached the edge of the yard, Danny turned and looked back towards the woods. He knew he'd done something good, something fine. Although he didn't see it at the time, he was defining himself. Certainly, in the grand scheme, saving Fred seemed a small thing, but it is by such small things that the inner citadel of character is fashioned. He also knew that down there on the hillside was a spring pool, and in it swam "a little silver trout." He felt a sudden surge of joy, suspecting, indeed, this promised to be a splendid summer.

TWO

DANNY'S DANGEROUS GAME

And hardly a day has gone by when I haven't thought
About those sweet and shimmering, free-hearted years,
And I at the wheel of my jeep up in timberline country,
In summer, with fly rod, and food box, and blankets, and time.
— John Wickersham —

The Conrad family lived west of the Grays on Elm Circle. Mr. Conrad owned a 1949 Willys jeep. Recently, he'd bought a larger Willys station wagon for family camping trips, and he offered the jeep for sale. Russell thought it would be perfect for John, Danny's big brother. The jeep could crawl over rocks and logs, cross creeks, and carry John and his sister and brother into the mountain backcountry.

John, a redhead like his mom, was fearless and clever. Since he had a driver's license and drove the family Plymouth frequently, it was evident his dad considered him responsible. Trust was the glue that held the family together.

Grandma Ruth doted on John, and she also let him drive her car, a '41 Fort sedan with a V-8 engine, a car particularly prized by hot-rodders. Although not one himself, John relished the envy of his friends when he occasionally drove her car to school. It was clear Grandma trusted him as well.

Russell bought the jeep, and John would pay his dad back by doing all their yard work and the same for his grandma's house which was next door. Russell asked John for his word. John pledged it. Having struck the deal, John became the owner of a fine little truck. He called his jeep "Frances" and painted the name below the windshield.

Frances was eight years old, and her previous owners drove her hard and frequently refused to take no for an answer. Consequently, she needed mechanical attention to make her a safe ride. Eager to undertake the project, John needed two things: guidance and money. Russell agreed to bankroll the repairs, reasoning, since he'd already bought the jeep, it would be wise to ensure that his kids drove around in a safe vehicle.

Serendipity entered in the person of Ed Bartlett, the restaurant's storeroom manager and handyman. Ed had served as a navy radioman during the war and afterward worked for several years in the Border Patrol. John regarded Ed as the master of all crafts and trades, and in truth, Ed had the tinkerer's gift for being able to figure out almost any machine. He liked John and treated him as a younger brother. He would provide the guidance.

First on the list were good brakes. Trying to stop Frances when underway was a real adventure. After a thorough inspection, Ed shook his head balefully and told John, as a starter, the brake system would have to be replaced. In addition, other repairs were needed. In the evenings after work, Ed and John labored over the jeep. Ed was a patient man and not easily frustrated.

Problem by problem, they rehabilitated Frances. The brakes were replaced: new master cylinder, new wheel cylinders, new drums, new shoes and hardware. Next came the front axle. Both of the Bendix joints on the axle ends were played out so that Frances popped and jerked whenever asked to turn sharply.

The gears in the transmission and transfer case were sound and both operated smoothly. However, both boxes oozed gear oil nonstop, and the clutch disc was oil soaked and almost nonfunctional. Ed and John dropped the two gear boxes, resealed them, resurfaced the flywheel, and replaced the clutch.

The steering, almost laughably erratic, made it a chore to keep

Frances between the fences when driving down a gravel road at 30 mph. The two-man pit crew replaced the tie rod ends and the bell crank bearings. They then removed the play in the steering gear, set the toe-in of the wheels to factory specs, replaced the shock absorbers, and had the four bald tires retreaded allowing Frances to roll down the road straight and true.

Finally, they tackled the four-cylinder engine. Though small, the sixty horsepower engine was stout and nearly indestructible. In low gear, low range, Frances could climb a 45-degree slope. A tune-up replaced the spark plugs, the distributor points, and coil. They removed the one-barrel carburetor, disassembled and rebuilt it. Finally, fresh crankcase oil and a new oil filter finished the project. This transformation took about a week of late nights in the garage, but the results were amazing. It was almost as if Frances were a new truck. In addition, John became a passable shade-tree mechanic in the bargain.

During that summer, at every opportunity, the kids loaded up Frances with their camping gear and headed off to explore the Colorado Rockies. There were so many wonderful places: ghost towns, gold and silver mines, abandoned homesteads, and old railroad grades. Every time they returned, they added new treasures to the pile in the back of the garage. There were lanterns, railroad spikes, old newspapers, blue-glass bottles, padlocks, spectacles, shovels, jugs, all manner of wonderful stuff.

These trips into the Colorado backcountry were important for Danny. He learned about the history of the region, about the native plants and animals, and much about himself. He soon gained confidence as a mountain boy, acquiring grown-up skills. He learned how to choose a campsite, how to foretell weather in the patterns of passing clouds, and how to stay warm and dry during the frequent downpours. The wild trout of the mountains particularly interested Danny.

One such expedition began on a bright June day when John went shopping for some trout flies at Blick's Sporting Goods. An old fisherman, a regular at Blick's, told John about Wheeler Lake located among the peaks of the Park Range west of Fairplay. The man said a population of cutthroat trout remained in this remote lake. Cutthroats were the native trout of Colorado; however, these beautiful fish, once plentiful in the streams and rivers of the state, were now rare. In 1956, they could only be found in remote waters in the backcountry. Chasing down this rumor would be a great way to spend a summer day.

The kids' father was an accomplished fly fisherman, having learned as a boy when he lived beside the North Fork of the Gunnison River, and throughout his life it remained one of his greatest pleasures. When they were old enough, he taught the boys the movements of the cast, which are the Law and the Prophets of fly fishing, so to speak. On Danny's eighth birthday, Russell gave him a beautiful split bamboo fly rod. Near the cork grip, a decal spelled out "Silver Lake Fly Rod." Danny cherished it as his most prized possession. He loved the appearance and the names of trout flies. His favorites were the Royal Coachman and the Western Bee.

The following Saturday morning found John, Mary, and Danny in Frances, chugging across South Park toward the peaks of the Park Range. The jeep trail to Wheeler Lake branched off a gravel county road above Montgomery Reservoir. The trail proved difficult with a particularly harrowing stretch where two granite slabs made a V-shaped notch filled with jagged rocks. These formed loose ledges that rolled and tumbled under the tires. The jeep clawed over and through these obstacles, emerging triumphant at the top, but when John continued up the trail, Frances foundered. Suddenly, the frame rails were banging on nearly every large rock. Something wasn't right.

John came to a halt and killed the engine. Walking around the jeep, he discovered that the right front tire was flat. Undoubtedly, he'd punctured it on the jagged rocks of the notch. He got back in, fired the engine up, and limped a few yards to a grassy bench where he could get her off the trail.

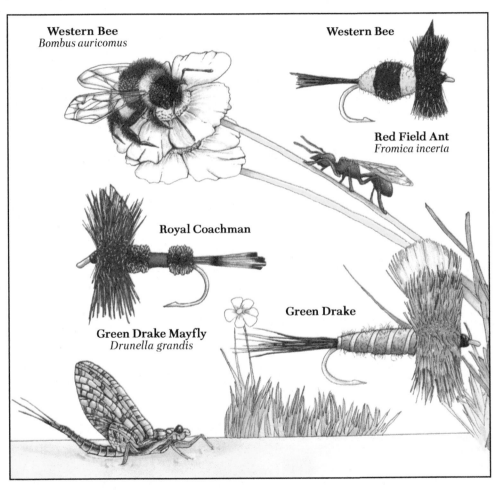

Western Bee
Bombus auricomus

Western Bee

Red Field Ant
Fromica incerta

Royal Coachman

Green Drake

Green Drake Mayfly
Drunella grandis

Trout Flies and Insects

"I'll have to put on the spare," he said to Mary and Danny. "Why don't you guys get out and scout around. You could check out the mine buildings we passed a couple hundred yards back."

The chore was difficult because of the rocky uneven ground, but when the kids returned in a half hour, Frances was back on four good tires.

"Okay, let's saddle up," Mary said, eager to press on toward the lake.

"I don't think we should," countered John. "It would be foolish to drive three more miles deeper into the mountains without a spare tire. If we blew out another tire, we'd be up the proverbial tributary without the proper means of propulsion."

Danny cocked his head and squinted at John. "What does that mean? What's a proverbial tributary?"

Mary rolled her eyes. "He means we'd be up the creek without a paddle. Everybody knows that."

"Well, I don't know it," said Danny.

"That's because you're not a body," Mary retorted in a matter-of-fact tone.

"Wait a minute!" Danny tried to object, frowning in confusion.

"You don't become a body until you're fourteen," she explained.

John raised his fly rod case and tapped Danny lightly on the shoulder. "I dub you an honorary body. There, that takes care of it."

Danny laughed and play-punched his brother. He realized that Mary and John were joking with him.

"Well, now I'm somebody!" he said proudly, standing stiffly like a soldier with his fly rod case at right-shoulder arms.

⟐

Having loaded their knapsacks with their fishing gear and rain shells, the three set out on the hike to Wheeler Lake. Mary wasn't happy; this hike hadn't been part of the plan. For a while, the trail threaded its way through a lodge pole pine forest, climbing ever higher. Soon they were up into the timberline tundra where the trees thinned out and the landscape became a series of grassy alps with rushing spring creeks and clumps of columbine, fireweed, paintbrush, and monkshood scattered about.

As they hiked along, a Gray Jay followed them, gliding from tree to tree, begging for food. Local people called these birds "Camp Robbers" because they congregated around camps hoping for handouts. Danny carried a packet of soda crackers in his knapsack, and, from time to time, he threw a cracker to the jay and laughed at the antics of the big bird that had become their travelling companion.

After several hard miles, Mary's patience wore thin. "How much farther is it to the lake, Johnny?" she complained. "I think we've walked ten miles."

"Be patient," responded John, "It's right around the corner; we're almost there."

"That's what you always say just to make me keep on walking. I'm telling you, I'm about finished." Mary sat down on a rock and folded her arms in protest.

Danny was tired as well, but he didn't want John to know. If he complained, John would tease him about being a little kid. All three understood these outings weren't for little kids.

John soon outdistanced Mary and Danny. When he crossed the top of a small rise, he turned and shouted. "Come on, you guys! I can see the lake. It's beautiful."

Forgetting their weariness, Mary and Danny struggled to the ridgetop. The lake nestled in a glacial cirque at the foot of several high peaks, the remains of a glacier that melted thousands of years ago. Large boulders and a snowfield edged much of the lake, but the outlet stream meandered through a grassy meadow lush with wildflowers. If cutthroat trout survived here, they lived in a world of indescribable beauty.

Quickly the boys set up their fly rods. "Tie on a Green Drake, Danny," said John. "It's a good imitation of the mayflies the trout are taking."

Much of the lake was hard to fish because the boulder-strewn shoreline made back casting difficult. However, the open grassy banks around the outlet were ideal. High lakes can be very temperamental. A fisherman can flail away all day and not get a single strike. Suddenly the lake can turn, and he can get a strike on nearly every cast.

On this day, the trout of Wheeler Lake were unusually finicky. Danny had no luck, but John finally caught a fourteen-inch female cutthroat in lustrous spawning colors. The gill plates and the slashes under the throat were a brilliant crimson, giving rise to the name. Danny examined the fish carefully so as to see the differences between it and Fred. It appeared similar to rainbow trout, but the crimson around its head and throat was distinctive. Once Danny understood the difference clearly, John released the fish, and it dove into the depths of the lake.

Eventually, the boys pulled their lines off the water. They'd accomplished their goal; they found this lake and saw these handsome fish. Besides, Mary chafed at being left out because she didn't fish, and she badgered her brothers to look for other interesting things to do.

"Come on," she said, "let's see if we can find souvenirs to take home. There are bound to be old mines around here."

Earlier, John had noticed a pile of yellow waste rock up on the mountainside that usually marked a mine, and he pointed it out to Mary and Danny.

"We might find some old buildings if we hike up there," he said.

"Maybe we'll find some stuff the miners left behind," Danny enthused, "like a coffee can full of gold nuggets!"

John laughed. "You're hopeless, Danny."

The climb up to the mine was steep. In several spots they were forced to climb hand over hand.

"Be careful," warned John. "Try not to dislodge rocks. A rolling rock could hurt someone below you."

"Stop nagging," Mary shot back. "We can take care of ourselves."

When they reached the mine, they found the ruins of several buildings and the wreckage of mining machinery strewn around. Behind one of the buildings, a mine shaft yawned darkly before them. The three stepped gingerly into the gloomy tunnel, John leading with a flashlight. In the dim light, they could see a miner's lantern, a pick, a shovel, and several mysterious wooden boxes.

"What do you think is in those boxes?" asked Danny. "Maybe it's gold!"

"I don't think so. It's probably just junk the miners left behind," said John. Then he brushed the heavy dust off the top of one of the boxes in order to examine its contents. "I'll be damned!" John blurted out. "These are boxes of dynamite!"

One of the boxes sat partially open, and Danny pried back the top to look in.

"Don't mess around with that stuff, Danny!" John warned. "It could be dangerous!"

Inside the box, the sticks of dynamite looked like brown paper tubes. They were layered like Lincoln Logs, row atop row. Danny was already making plans.

"Look, John. The label says it came from a mining supply store in Fairplay. It's dated 1906. This dynamite is fifty years old; it can't be very dangerous anymore. This is really neat! Let's take some back with us."

"Not on your life," John quickly responded. "It's too dangerous. Besides, how would we get any of it down the mountain?"

"We could slide a box in front of us as we climb down," Danny answered readily.

At this point, Mary entered the dispute. "It would be stupid to fiddle with dynamite. What would Mom and Dad say if they knew what we're doing? I'm with John; that makes it two to one, little brother. You lose."

On the way back down the trail to the jeep, Danny pouted. He didn't like it when John and Mary ganged up on him. If they didn't want any dynamite, they didn't have to take any, but he could see no reason why he shouldn't be able to salvage such a spectacular souvenir.

Back at Frances, the kids built a small fire to roast hot dogs. While John nursed the fire into life, Mary and Danny cut several branches from a streamside willow for roasting sticks. As they prepared to eat, an old, shabbily dressed man came walking down the trail leading a pack mule. The mule carried two panniers with a pick and shovel tied on top. The man wore a sweat-stained hat with a leather loop that hung under his chin whiskers. His face and hands were deeply tanned and wrinkled, and his eyes were knowing and kind. He stopped and greeted the kids.

"Howdy, children. What brings you up into these hills?"

John introduced himself and his siblings. The old man shook the hand of each with great formality. "I'm honored to meet you," he said. "I'm a friend to anyone who loves these mountains, and I can see you children do. By the way, do you have another hot dog for this old man?"

His name was Tony Perce, and he was a longtime prospector. For an hour, he charmed the kids with stories of the old days when miners dug for silver and gold in these mountains. At one point Tony told a story about miners dying in an explosion. He explained that one of them mishandled the dynamite they were using. Upon hearing this, Danny excitedly spilled the story of their find at the old mine, how he wanted to bring some dynamite home, and how John and Mary wouldn't let him. He made a particular point about the date on the box and the age of the dynamite. He concluded it couldn't be dangerous.

Tony sat silently for a moment and stared into the fire. Then he spoke very solemnly. "Danny, today you almost died. That date on the box told the miners the dynamite would be unstable a few years after 1906; it could easily explode on its own. Just picking up a stick probably would have set it off. If you got so far as to slide a box down the mountain, it surely would have blown up. Had those boxes blown up, it would have shattered tons and tons of rock and blown you kids to bits.

Tony's words stunned Danny. He looked at John and Mary, and then tears began rolling down his cheeks. Tony reached out and patted Danny's knee. "It's all right," he said. "You're fine. That's all that matters."

───※◆※───

That night, lying in the comfort and safety of his bed, Danny thought about the events of the day. As he usually did, he made an examination of his conscience. He realized he'd been stupid. He'd acted like a little kid. He, Mary, and John were spared a terrible fate.

Danny thought about the lesson learned, about the fragility of life, and about the frightening consequences that can result from thoughtless choices. The world, he realized, had many pitfalls that are not at all obvious. He promised himself he wouldn't rush so headlong into things and that he'd be more thoughtful about the path of his life. Danny grew up some that night.

THREE

RUSSELL BUYS AN AIRPLANE

Oh! I have slipped the surly bonds of Earth,
And danced the skies on laughter-silvered wings;
Sunward I've climbed, and joined the tumbling mirth
Of sun-split clouds ...
— John Magee —

One afternoon in late June, Russell told Louise and the kids something quite amazing: he'd bought an airplane.

Louise wasn't amused. "Our family needs many things much more than an airplane. To begin, John will be going away to college in a year."

"All I ask is that you keep an open mind, come see the plane and go for a ride. If you still think it's a mistake, I'll sell it," Russell offered apologetically. He knew better than to argue with his redheaded wife when her eyes flashed.

Of course, there's usually a story behind every story. Russell learned to fly in 1927 when he was in high school back in Grand Junction. At the primitive strip that served as the airport, the one airworthy plane dusted crops in the Grand Valley. The owner of the plane was a skilled pilot and aircraft mechanic.

In addition, he owned a Curtiss Jenny with a broken engine that sat forlorn in the weeds beside the hangar. In the indefinite future,

Curtiss JN-4 "Jenny"

he intended to make it airworthy. For a variety of reasons, he could never find the time. When Russell and his pals offered to repair the plane, he sold it to them for a modest sum and even agreed to oversee their mechanical work. Since the boys were skilled mechanics, having souped up their Model T Fords, they made quick work of rebuilding the Jenny's engine. It had a solid airframe, but they needed to repair numerous small tears in the fabric covering the fuselage and wings which were then given several coats of shellac. After successfully starting and breaking in the engine, a careful rehab of all the control cables prepared the old girl to soar again.

Actual flying became the next step. The pilot gave the boys a couple of hours of ground school, teaching them how the manipulation of the controls produced changes in the attitude of the airplane. The logic was fairly straightforward – throttle in and out, dive and climb, turn and bank. Then the boys drew straws, and Russell drew the short one. He would go first.

Before flying, the old pilot explained exactly what they'd be doing and how things would go. First would be taking off. They'd have to throttle up the engine, pull back gently on the stick, and climb slowly. Once aloft, he said, they'd practice the various movements of the stick and pedals for about an hour. When the Jenny ran low on gas, they'd check the red-and-white wind sock to see the wind direction, line up on the runway, keep the plane level, throttle back, and ease her down onto the ground.

Then came the real thing. He went up with Russell several times, coaching him in the use of the controls and explaining the response of the airplane. When, in the pilot's judgment, Russell demonstrated competence, he made a solo flight. He'd become a bona fide pilot.

The two other boys, however, couldn't get the knack. One did a ground loop and broke the propeller. The other immediately lost interest. Russell ended up as the sole proprietor of the Jenny after a complicated exchange of money, goods, and promises.

For the next several summers, he barnstormed around western Colorado and eastern Utah, taking the locals up for rides at county fairs and church picnics. When the Great Depression hit, Russell sold his beloved plane. He remembered this time as a golden age, and, in truth, he never completely outgrew it. During his lifetime, he logged 15,000 hours of flying.

Russell belonged to a unique generation of American men. Born in the early twentieth century, they knew and lived among Civil War veterans. Many of their grandfathers served under arms during the Indian Wars. In the Grand Valley where Russell lived, people still talked about Butch Cassidy and the Hole in the Wall Gang. Like their fathers and grandfathers, these men grew up to be rugged individuals and risk-takers. Russell had been what would today be called a "free-range" child. His grandpa's farm on the banks of the North Fork of the Gunnison River was truly a boy's paradise.

He illustrated this spirit of creative independence when his mother, Ruth, contracted the Spanish flu. For several days, she hovered between life and death. She couldn't keep any food or water down and was wasting away. Sick with fear and frustrated by the doctor's inability to help her, he decided to take matters into his own hands. Russell went down to the river with a cane pole and caught several small bullhead catfish. He knew his mom loved catfish filets battered and fried in butter, so he prepared a meal for her, convinced this would break the grip of the flu. To his great joy, she immediately improved, getting up and around several days thereafter.

There's a wonderful picture of Russell in the family album at the age of ten. He wears a large newsboy cap, a nondescript shirt, ragged overalls, and is barefooted. He has his Winchester .22 pump on his shoulder, and he is accompanied by his constant boyhood companion, a rangy collie named Bobby. As the only child of a widow and living far from town, he was mostly on his own. The photograph is a memorable tableau: Russell and Bobby stand on a caving bank above the river, clearly setting off on the day's adventure.

Thus, in the early summer of 1956, when an ad for a Cessna 170 appeared in the *Gazette-Telegraph*, he couldn't help himself: Russell would go flying again. He knew from his own experience, if Louise would go for a ride with him in his new plane, she'd fall in love with flight just as he had many years before. When the next Sunday dawned cool and bright, the family piled into the Plymouth and headed for Peterson Field. Once there, Russell proudly showed the family his new baby, a red and white Cessna 170. The kids ran around and under, climbed into and out of the beautiful plane.

"Does it have machine guns?" Danny asked excitedly.

His dad laughed. "No, Danny. Only Air Force fighters are armed. This little plane is a pleasure craft, not a P-51 Mustang."

The kids waited in the terminal lobby while Russell and Louise set out on their maiden voyage in the Cessna. The plane taxied out to the runway. After getting cleared for takeoff, it sped down the runway headed west into the wind, accelerated quickly, and leaped into the air. Russell waggled the wings to show off for the kids. Soon the plane was only a small dot against the blue sky until it disappeared altogether.

Danny turned to John and asked with concern, "What if they crash?"

John, ever the expert, dismissed the question. "They'll just bail out and parachute to the ground," he said confidently. "Don't worry. They'll be fine."

It seemed forever, but it took only thirty minutes before the plane came gliding out of the eastern sky toward the runway. It descended slowly like a falling leaf, bobbing this way and that as it settled into a glide path toward the runway. The wheels touched down and the tail dropped onto its wheel, making a perfect landing.

When Louise climbed down from the cabin of the plane, her face glowed. The kids could tell she was thrilled by the experience of her first flight, having "wheeled and soared and swung, high in the sunlit silence" as John Magee once described the feeling. The Grays now owned an airplane.

Russell promised to take the kids for a ride in the Cessna the following Sunday. When the day came, they were almost sick with excitement on the drive out to Peterson Field. For his part, Danny prepared himself thoroughly to go flying. He wore a leather fighter pilot's helmet and goggles given to him by an uncle after the war. In the car he practiced his specialty, making gun noises. As soon as Russell parked the car, Danny began his own flying. With his helmet and goggles on, he imagined himself a P-51, all the while shooting his mouth machine gun at imaginary enemy fighters.

After Russell went through the preflight check and gassed up, they boarded the plane. John sat in the copilot's seat next to his dad. Mary and Danny sat behind them. The kids were fascinated by all the details of the cabin, and they peppered their dad with questions. He patiently explained the controls, how the wheel and the rudder pedals worked, how the throttle made the engine run fast or slow, and the basic functions of the airspeed indicator, the altimeter, and the compass.

"Yeah, Dad, but what makes it fly?" Danny asked with a sense of urgency.

"The air rushing under the wings is stronger than the air rushing over the wings. It pushes up on the wings, and that's called lift," he explained. "The faster the air rushes, the greater the lift."

Suddenly, the radio crackled in the cabin, full of information from the tower: wind speed, wind direction, weather – all the things Russell needed to know in order to take off. Last of all, the tower cleared them for takeoff. None of the three had ever flown in an airplane. All had a woozy feeling in their stomachs.

"Where are the parachutes, Dad?" asked John, trying to seem unconcerned. "We need to know in case the engine dies."

"Private aircraft don't carry parachutes, John. Because the safety record of these planes is so good, parachutes aren't really necessary."

"Smarty pants, Johnny," Mary whispered, just loud enough to be heard by everyone.

Their dad taxied into position at the end of the runway. With the brakes on, he ran up the engine speed. The roar both scared and thrilled them. The Cessna shook and vibrated. Finally, he released the brakes. The plane leapt forward and sped down the runway. The kids all grabbed the nearest solid thing to hold onto. John looked out the window and watched the concrete runway rush under the plane's wheels. Mary shut her eyes tightly. Danny thought he was surely going to die.

Gradually, everything became smooth and quiet. They were floating almost as if in a dream. The land dropped away, the buildings grew smaller, and the airport receded into the distance. They were actually flying.

In a few minutes, they were miles east of town over the endless sweep of prairie that reached all the way to Kansas. It made a perfect backdrop for Russell. He thrilled the kids with some mild aerobatics. First, he put the plane through a Lazy Eight consisting of one banking turn, a cross over its own path, and another banking turn into the original path.

Next, he did a Wingover. Russell pushed the plane into a steep climb until it almost stalled. Then he nosed over, banked, and resumed level flight in the opposite direction. Finally, for a big finish, he did an Immelmann, named after a World War I German pilot, climbing into a half-roll, then leveling out again so the plane reverses direction. These swoops and dives thrilled the kids, reminding them of the scary rides at the carnival that came through town every summer.

"Wow, Dad. That was really something!" John said. Though not considered good form for a seventeen-year-old boy to show enthusiasm, he abandoned all pretense. "How did you learn to fly like that?" It's just like in the movies. The only thing missing was a Jap Zero on our tail!"

"Can you fly at night?" Mary wondered. "How could you know which direction you're going?"

"My instruments tell me the attitude and direction of the plane. Even if I couldn't see anything but stars, I could still tell if the plane were level and which direction it faced."

Danny remained stupefied by the experience. Try as he might, he couldn't think of anything to say. Finally, he said, "Dad, you're a really good pilot. That's all I've got to say."

When the plane reached 11,500 ft., Russell asked the kids, "Would you like to fly all the way around Pikes Peak?"

"That would be great!" John responded.

Mary chimed in, "That would be swell!" using a word she'd heard her dad say many times.

Not to be outdone, Danny said, "That would be *cool!*"

Russell winked at John. "Where did you hear that word, Danny?"

"A guy on the radio said rock and roll music is *cool.*"

The others laughed.

"Do you even know what rock and roll music is, Danny?" Mary queried.

"Okay," countered Danny, "I think it would be *muy simpático.*"

Russell, John, and Mary laughed at Danny's reply. Flying around Pikes Peak would be very nice, indeed.

As the Cessna bore west, they could see how Pikes Peak dominated the landscape with its forested skirts flowing off in all directions. It was visible from the Kansas border, over a hundred miles away. The Grays looked out the windows of the plane as it buzzed along in the high, thin atmosphere.

Within twenty minutes, they could see Cripple Creek and its neighboring town, Victor, spread out on the barren slopes below Pikes Peak. The views from the plane astonished the kids. To the south marched the great Sangre de Cristo Range, to the west rose the Collegiate Peaks, and the peaks of Rocky Mountain National Park lay to the north. In addition, there were countless small, interesting details – ranches, roads, creeks, rivers, and vast, sweeping forests.

"Do you see the little town on the highway below us?" asked Russell. "That's Divide. Fred Wilson's trout farm is on West Creek. I think that's West Creek out the right window. See how it runs through the five lakes?"

Danny pressed his face to the window and squinted against the bright sunlight. "I see them, Dad! That's where Fred came from."

In his mind's eye, Danny could see Mr. Wilson scooping Fred out of one of the lakes into a bucket, taking him down to Colorado Springs to the restaurant, and Danny himself saving Fred from a cruel fate.

"When I bought your jeep from Mr. Conrad, John, he told me about a fishing hole in the hills north of Divide called Rule Creek. He said it would be a great spot for you to take your jeep. Let's see if we can spot it."

The kids were all peering intensely out the windows when their dad said, "I think that's it in the valley ahead."

The valley was yellow, edged by the green of forest. Down the middle of the valley wound a tiny blue thread with blue beads strung along it.

"There's Rule Creek. See the beaver ponds? Mr. Conrad said it's his secret place, but he gave me the directions to get there."

Immediately, John imagined himself in Frances, shifting gears, working the clutch and brakes, crawling down the mountainside to reach this secret place. "It would be so cool to drive that road," he said.

In half an hour, they were back over Colorado Springs. When they reached Peterson Field, Russell lined up with the runway the control tower had assigned him. As they glided down, the radio crackled, the plane swayed back and forth, and the ground rushed up at them. Danny could almost see the headline in tomorrow's *Gazette-Telegraph*: 'Local Family Killed in Plane Crash!' But, before he knew it, the plane touched down, the tail dropped down on its wheel, and they were rolling along the concrete runway. The three kids began gushing all at once about the thrilling experience of their first airplane ride. It had been *really cool!*

Once home, Danny walked down to Fred's spring. He sat silently on the grassy bank, still stunned with wonder at what he'd seen from the plane. The things made by people were so small. Highways were just lines; buildings were little dots. He remembered how roads and railway lines crisscrossed the landscape. He wondered why people had chosen those particular paths. Where were they all going? If he were down there, where would he go, which path would he follow? He couldn't even see individual people, as though they no longer existed.

At that moment, a faint breeze arose and brushed across Danny's face. He raised his hand to feel the movement and blew a breath across his hand. This was the same air upon which he'd floated today. He realized the world swims in an ocean of air, subtle and transparent. It startled him, something so obvious yet mysterious. This was the first time in his life he'd consciously encountered the vast. He began to understand how limitless, how far-flung was the world, and that he was but a small speck upon the great blue planet.

FOUR

MARY BESTS THE LITTLE DISHPAN GANG

If somebody pushes, you push back;
You show your enemy that you're tough.
~ Patricia Bunn ~

It continued to be an amazing summer. John's jeep was a freedom machine, and nearly every week brought a new adventure. The kids' heads swam with ideas about new places to go, new perils to face. How could they top finding a stash of dynamite? What could be more thrilling than buzzing along at 12,000 feet, admiring the landscape from a plane? There seemed to be no end of possibilities.

The kids' daily routine often included a visit to Fred in the morning before they went to work at the restaurant. As time permitted, Danny improved the spring pool. He spaded it out to deepen it and brought watercress plants up from the lake. They soon took hold and spread around the edges. Finally, he placed a big rock in the pool to provide some shade and safety. On their visits to Fred, the kids sat on the grass and tossed pieces of dry bread on the water. Instantly, Fred would break through the glassy surface and pounce on the bread.

After several weeks, Fred grew accustomed to their visits. As soon as they appeared beside the spring pool, he darted back and forth from under the rock ledge. Danny remembered Mr. Wilson's joke about taking the little trout to bed. If he could figure out a way to keep Fred in some water, he thought, he probably could take him to bed.

Danny worried constantly. Raccoons and other wild animals might happen upon the spring pool and catch Fred. He realized he couldn't control this danger, so he tried not to dwell on it. The other very real danger, however, came from people. Someone might discover it. The kids who lived on the nearby roads were friends. They knew the Grays owned the hillside woods, and they wouldn't go there by themselves. The real danger would come from across the valley.

The other side of the valley marked the territory of the Little Dishpan Gang. A metal dishpan hung from a tree limb in front of their ramshackle clubhouse. They banged on it like a dinner bell whenever they entered or left. The gang numbered about ten members, but three boys made up the core – the Gates brothers, Geno and Nick, and their best pal, Inky Davis. The boys in the gang were dangerous; at least that's what all the other kids thought. They wore their hair slicked back like the actors in movie magazines. Each one carried a pack of cigarettes rolled up in the sleeve of his T-shirt. They all wore aviator sunglasses. In their own minds, they were fearsome.

The children's world in a small Colorado town in 1956 was rough and tumble. The kids were shaped by World War II, the great event of their time, and in a hundred ways their lives reflected that conflict. Millions of American boys went to war as seventeen and eighteen-year olds. The average age of B-17 pilots was twenty-three. Those who survived returned to civilian life with a definite swagger and derring-do mirrored in movies like *The Wild Ones*. By the fifties, these attitudes had seeped into teen culture. The appearance of rock and roll music, movies like *The Blackboard Jungle* and *Rebel without a Cause* energized the high schoolers of America.

At the supper table, during his sophomore year, John gave the Gray family a wide-eyed account of the shocking misbehavior of a fellow student. One of the boys in his class, having recently seen *The Blackboard Jungle*, addressed Sister Frances Louise as "Teach" mimicking one of the actors in the movie. Needless to say, this lapse into hooliganism wasn't well received.

Mary lived in that world, and, as a result, she was fearless and resolute. She expected no quarter from her brothers and insisted on parity with them in all matters. In particular, she would brook no condescension from boys. Complementing these traits, she was also balanced in her judgment. Mary spoke with the voice of reason in all their adventures, and, most importantly, she was tough, one of the many reasons her brothers admired her. She never asked for special treatment. She could take care of herself. She always did her part.

It wasn't easy. Being caught between two boys fated her to be a tomboy. But, by and large, she embraced the masculine ethos that dominated her family. There were few organized sports for kids before high school, but the Gray kids all loved the pickup baseball games of summer and the pond hockey that came with the winter ice. One could always find Mary right in the thick of things. In all these matters, she gave no quarter and asked for none.

"Tough" was the highest accolade one kid could give to another. In their world, a reputation for toughness provided protection from the manifold torments children regularly visited upon one another. If you were thought to be tough, for the most part you were given wagon room by other kids. How you acquired this perception of toughness resulted from what kids called "sticking up" – defending yourself, brothers, sisters, and friends. One stuck up for someone else by taking his part in a dispute, by defending him from bullying, or by simply refusing to be pushed around. When Mary and Danny set out on a hike on a bright July Saturday, Mary's toughness would be tested.

The day dawned bright and beautiful, with a deep blue sky and towering cumulus clouds over the prairie. They decided to go to the lake first before visiting Fred. In many respects, the lake in the valley behind their home centered their outdoor activities. For example, the lake had an excellent population of panfish, and the boys frequently honed their casting skills on them.

In the winter, the lake ice froze thickly enough for skating from early December until mid-January. John played center on the St. Mary's

Prairie Rattlesnake
Crotalus viridis

The Path to the Spring

hockey team, and on many cold winter mornings, he and Mary would skate for an hour before school. Weekends during the hockey season usually featured a skating party with a bonfire, hot chocolate, laughter, and lots of flirting. John's circle of friends, both boys and girls, hated to see the ice begin to weaken with the gradually warming weather. On several occasions, they pushed the limit, and on one notorious late January Saturday, a big scrum of players, including a goalie in full pads and the goal, went through the ice.

On this particular July Saturday, Danny carried the army surplus knapsack his dad had given him. Russell told him it was identical to the one he'd used during the war. This day, he stashed peanut butter sandwiches and two bottles of pop in his knapsack. After their visit to the lake, he and Mary would have a picnic beside the spring pool.

As the two walked across the rattlesnake glade on the path to the lake, Danny spotted a recently shed snakeskin. He could still see the rattlesnake scale pattern. This would be a fine thing to put on the wall of his room, so he tucked it carefully into his knapsack. When they approached the lake, they heard strange noises. First came a *whoomp* followed by voices and laughter. After a couple of minutes, the same thing happened again. Mary and Danny had no idea what was happening, but when the lake came in sight, they understood. Several boys were firecracker fishing, which explained both the *whoomp* and the laughter.

The boys tied cherry bombs onto rocks, lit the fuses, and threw them into the lake. The fuses burned under water, followed by an explosion, a gusher of water, and the loud *whoomp*. Fish floated to the surface of the lake stunned by the explosion. After scooping them up with a long-handled net, the boys threw the bluegill and sunfish into a pail and repeated the process.

"That's really chicken," whispered Danny. "The fish have no chance!"

"That's the Little Dishpan Gang," Mary whispered. "Let's go to the stream and follow it back up to Fred's pool. This is none of our business, and we don't want them to see us."

When Mary and Danny reached the sandbar at the inlet, out

of sight of the gang, they felt safer, and they sat down to rest for a moment. Suddenly, the boys burst out of the willows that sheltered the sandbar. Mary and Danny were startled and jumped to their feet. The boys stood in a half circle in front of them. Danny felt surrounded, and fear made his heart beat fast. He remembered what his dad once told him – there's no shame in fear; you just have to be brave.

Pumped up with strut and bluster, Nick began taunting Mary. He didn't get far. Mary easily parried his insults with her own clever taunts. "Is that the best you can do?" she asked, her voice dripping sarcasm.

Being a bully, Nick enjoyed intimidating younger kids. He and his pals were accustomed to dominance and quite unused to such spirited resistance. They lifted weights in order to increase the impact of their physical presence, concentrating their efforts on upper-body exercises so as to show off their arms and shoulders. This cultivated musculature was a scary prospect to a typical twelve or thirteen year old.

Many of Mary's friends, boys and girls, would be reduced to tears at this point. As he loomed over Mary, the two were a striking contrast of types. Nick moved casually from pose to pose, each one carefully calculated to display his physical superiority to her. She stood stock still, squarely in front of him, locking his eyes with hers, and bristling defiance.

At this point, Geno entered the lists. "Shut your mouth, or I'll slap it shut it for you," he blurted out, trying to counter Mary's courage.

"If you slap me, I'll be the last girl you'll ever slap. My brother, Johnny, will come looking for you, and he'll beat the daylights out of you all!"

Geno sputtered and glared at Mary with his fists clenched. He couldn't do anything. He was the victim of an unwritten code among kids that even the Little Dishpan Gang obeyed: boys don't hit girls. They'd have to get Danny. While Mary's attention focused on Geno, Nick glanced knowingly at Inky and then crept behind Danny. Danny caught this movement out of the corner of his eye, but pretended not to notice. Then, Inky stepped toward Danny, holding up his fists in front of himself like a boxer.

"I'm going to whip you good!" yelled Inky, mustering up all the menace he could.

Danny knew what to expect. Nick and Inky were using a bully's trick he'd seen before. When Nick got down on all fours, Inky would charge Danny, who would fall backwards over Nick. Then, Inky would pounce on him and pummel him until Danny cried "Uncle!"

When Inky rushed at him swinging his fists, Danny stepped aside and grabbed Inky's shirt with both hands. As Inky lunged past, Danny heaved him over Nick's back. Inky tumbled awkwardly, hit the ground with a thud, and rolled into a patch of prickly pear cactus.

Instantly, Inky jumped up and looked at the many cactus spines sticking into his arm and leg. With tears streaming down his face, he yelled "Ow! It really hurts, you guys! I'm going home!"

"¡*Qué lástima!*" said Danny, now puffed up from his unexpected triumph. "What a shame!"

At this point, Geno and Nick realized their plan hadn't gone well. They looked at each other and then into their pail.

"Come on," Nick said grumpily, "let's get some more fish."

As they started toward the woods, Mary couldn't pass up the chance to pull on their noses one more time. "Not many fish up in the trees," she called after them.

"We're not looking in the trees, stupid," growled Nick. "We're going up this creek. There may be a few fish in it."

Danny was startled out of his elation over the fight. He needed to do something fast, or Nick and Geno would find Fred, catch him, and kill him.

"I wouldn't go up there if I were you," he warned them, "because that hillside is *infested* with rattlesnakes."

His dad had used that word when describing the black widow spiders in their garden tool shed, and he thought it was a strong word. He reached into his knapsack and pulled out the snakeskin. Assuming a serious tone, Danny told them his family called the snake Big Sam. Furthermore, he said, the snake bit the family dog, Junior, just a few days ago, and the dog had rolled over and died.

Nick and Geno looked at the snakeskin for a moment, turned back toward the sandbar, and slouched sullenly past Mary and Danny.

Mary couldn't resist. "Oh, boys!" she called after them. They turned around and looked at her. "Bye, bye," she chirped, waving her hand back and forth in an exaggerated way.

———⊷◦⊷———

It would be difficult to underestimate the importance of toughness in the adolescent culture of those times. Mary had it, and she ranked right up there with John. Boys established their toughness typically through sports and fighting. John played on the St. Mary's hockey team, and he had four of his front teeth knocked out during a game. Toughness was a family thing.

On many occasions, Louise admonished her kids to stick up for one another. She spoke out of her own historical experience. During her childhood in east Denver, the Ku Klux Klan had burned a cross in front of her home because her family was Irish Catholic. This sort of hatred and abuse were commonplace in those days. Louise was definitely tough, and she imparted this to her children. Her toughness wasn't showy. Instead, it was a quiet strength that shone in her eyes. The Little Dishpan Gang saw it in Mary's eyes, too, which is why they backed down. This episode became Mary's signature triumph. When family stories were told at Christmas or other ceremonial occasions, everyone always insisted on hearing about the time Mary bested the Little Dishpan Gang.

———⊷◦⊷———

Later, by Fred's pool, where they were enjoying their picnic lunch, Danny said admiringly, "Mary, you're really tough."

"You're pretty tough, too, Danny. You stood up to Inky; that took real courage. Besides, I loved the story you told them about a rattlesnake named Big Sam. Where did you get that idea?"

"Somehow, I just had to save Fred. Dad once said 'All's fair in love and war,' and it seemed to me this was war. Anyway, that big snake needed a name. I'll make it up to Junior. He can sleep on my bed tonight," he said with a laugh. "Listen, Mary, I made up a poem:

'There goes Inky down the road,
Jumping like a little hop toad.
I think I know what makes him dance,
He has stickers in his pants!'"

Both Mary and Danny laughed happily as they walked across the rattlesnake glade on the way back home. Danny was entering into a new relationship with his sister. Until now, he accorded her a healthy respect based on the sheer fact she had two years on him. In the world of children, age is a huge advantage. Because of that respect, Danny gave deference to Mary in disputes, the offering of opinions, and such. But his newfound attitude grew out of affection. He was really proud of her.

The boys of the Little Dishpan Gang genuinely frightened Danny, but they didn't frighten Mary. As a result, in his eyes, Mary's stature dramatically increased. He looked at her as they walked along, and he realized he began to see her anew. She is my sister, he thought to himself, *my sister.*

FIVE

THE SECRET ROAD

Glory be to God for dappled things —
For skies of couple-colour as a brinded cow;
For rose-moles all in stipple upon trout that swim;
— Gerard M. Hopkins —

The Colorado mountains were much more densely populated in the late nineteenth century than in 1956. Mining camps sprawled in nearly every valley, and mines clung to the steep slopes of many peaks. For example, Leadville had a population in excess of 30,000 at the height of its boom and boasted electric street cars and service by three railroads. It came to an end when the silver market crashed in 1893.

Federal law required the Government to buy all domestically produced silver at an inflated price. The intent of the law was to stimulate the economy during a post-war depression by creating a far-flung silver mining industry throughout the West. When the international price fell to half of the domestic price, the government simply couldn't sustain the enormous drain on the treasury any longer. Overnight, the western silver mines closed. Not only did this devastate Colorado, but other western states as well. As a result, there occurred a precipitous decline in the population of mountain towns. Most of the smaller, more remote camps were abandoned and became ghost towns. Grass and wildflowers reclaimed meadows that once thronged with wagon traffic and cursing teamsters. Now, the only sounds were bird song and the wind.

Such extensive settlement had led to the construction of thousands of miles of roads. Most of these were marginal and primitive at best, and when the remote mining camps were abandoned, the roads became overgrown and forgotten. The marketing of the Willys CJ2A to the civilian population after the war changed all that. These mechanical mules were identical to the wartime jeeps so beloved by U.S. soldiers; they could negotiate with relative ease these old, long abandoned roads. If you owned a jeep, either a Willys or war surplus, you could reach truly remote locales and enjoy complete solitude.

In 1957, for example, the Gray kids drove Frances to a lonesome ghost town and camped for three days without seeing another living soul. This was to change in the 1960s when large manufacturers entered the market with four-wheel drive trucks. In 1956, a man could drive his jeep over Tincup Pass and not see another vehicle. By 1975, there would be a steady stream of traffic there on any summer day.

Early in this revolution in back country travel, jeep owners prided themselves on being the first to cross a high mountain pass or reach a remote ghost town. Everyone had his secret places and guarded them closely. Thus, for John, Mary, and Danny, Mr. Conrad's story about a secret road to a prime fishing hole relatively close to Colorado Springs proved irresistible.

On an August weekend, Danny and John loaded their camping gear into Frances. Mary helped where she could. Since her gift was organizing, she patiently arranged the gear, thrown in the jeep by the boys, into an orderly whole. As she directed the process, she pointed out to her brothers that a good boss is half of the job.

They were going to Rule Creek, Mr. Conrad's secret place. It would be an ideal way to bid farewell to a splendid summer. According to him, the creek swarmed with trout, and very few people knew its location. He told the kids about an abandoned road that dropped off a ridge down into the creek valley. A rusty coffee can on a tree stump marked where it joined the gravel county road. Built back in the gold mining days, the road hadn't been used for many years. If

The Turnoff for the Secret Road

John wanted to drive his jeep down it, he should watch for the coffee can and turn off the gravel road into the woods. The faint remains of the old road would barely be visible.

Things happened exactly so. They found the can and turned into an aspen forest, following the traces of the old road. John coaxed Frances carefully over the rutted trail, climbing over rocky outcrops and splashing through the rushing creek. Once in the valley, they looked for a campsite close to a beaver pond. The beavers' stick-and-mud dams impounded a series of ponds. In the middle of them, the beavers had made lodges in which they lived. The ponds would be swarming with trout.

Having passed several small ponds, they came to the largest one, ideally situated in a wide part of the meadow. The edges were clear of willows, and they would provide ample room for the boys to cast with little danger of snagging their lines. Here would be the perfect camp. Slightly uphill from the pond, the kids pitched their army surplus pup tent in the shade of a grove of aspens, called "quakies" because their leaves rattle and click musically in the breeze.

Their bed rolls would be very comfortable on the flat, grassy ground. The rear of the tent could be closed though the front remained open. The kids liked this, because they could watch the moon and stars from their beds until they fell asleep. They knew the importance of having the open end of the tent face east. All the storms came from the west, and, in a west facing tent, a driving night rain would soak them. Several yards in front of the tent, John made a ring of stones for a campfire to cook supper when evening came.

The trout were rising to insects all over the beaver pond, dimpling its surface with small circles. John was an accomplished fly fisherman, and Danny was gaining skill. They began fishing, sending their lines singing through the air with their slender fly rods.

The fish in the beaver pond were mostly brook trout, although there were a few rainbows. Brook trout are surely the most beautiful of all the trout found in the Colorado mountains. Their sleek bodies glow in a riot of colors, with dark-green backs, golden sides, and orange bellies. They're covered with colored spots, and their orange fins are edged with a white stripe.

Technically, brook trout aren't true trout. They belong to a genus called *Salvelinus* and are more properly called char than trout. However, char and trout are so closely related that the only meaningful difference between the two is a matter of their teeth. For all intents and purposes, char and trout are indistinguishable.

Standing on a grassy point, Danny began having a problem with wind knots.

"What am I doing, Johnny? I keep tangling my fly up with my leader."

"That means your back cast isn't strong enough. Try pulling back really hard; let the line get all the way behind you before you throw it forward. That's the secret."

Danny followed John's advice, and soon his casts were shooting out cleanly and far.

"How many shall we keep?" shouted John, holding up the handsome brookie he'd just landed.

This question troubled Danny, although it hadn't bothered him on previous fishing trips. How could he keep these beautiful fish and let them die? He thought about Fred in the spring pool back home and how much the trout meant to him.

"I'm not going to keep any," he answered. "I'm going to free mine back into the pond."

Standing on the opposite bank, John looked at the trout in his dip net, thought for a moment, and carefully released the fish.

"You're right. We have plenty of food. We don't need to keep any fish for supper."

Just catching them seemed wonderful enough. If they handled the trout carefully, they wouldn't be harmed. That day, Danny became a catch-and-release fisherman, though he'd never heard that expression. Fred had changed Danny. He'd taught Danny all living things are precious.

Mary didn't fish. In her opinion fishing was for boys and beneath her.

Instead, she pursued her favorite interest – photography. She'd received a fine camera, an Argus 75, as a Christmas gift from Grandma Ruth, who also gave Mary a portrait lens that allowed her to take close-up pictures. Mary loved her camera. Mountain and prairie wildflowers were her favorite subjects. While the boys fished the beaver pond, she spent the day exploring the woods and the lush meadows searching out picturesque clumps of flowers.

She had the ideal camera for photographing wildflowers, a twin-lens reflex that allowed the photographer to look down into the viewfinder on the top of the camera. Mary mounted the camera on a small tripod. When she positioned it in front of an array of blossoms, she could frame and focus the image while kneeling down instead of having to lie on the ground to look through the viewfinder. At home she kept an album of her wildflower pictures. Here, amid this floral bounty, she hoped to find a lush tuft of columbine or perhaps some larkspur or Indian paintbrush. Perhaps she could add to her collection.

Although Mary lacked formal instruction, she had a natural sense of composition and design. She sought out shaded pockets of flowers where one or two blossoms might be isolated against the green surround. She learned by trial and error that the most pleasing images featured a strong, dominant subject. Whenever she showed her pictures to other people, she noticed that the ones which drew praise always had this kind of visual strength.

The delicacy and fragility of wildflowers particularly appealed to Mary. Come back tomorrow, and the mix of blossoms could be very different or perhaps gone altogether. She remembered several lines from a poem by Robert Herrick she'd learned in Sr. Cristella's English class. She loved it when these snatches of verse popped into her mind at unexpected moments. Savoring the words, she said,

> "Gather ye rosebuds while ye may,
> Old Time is still a-flying;
> And this same flower that smiles today
> Tomorrow will be dying."

In many respects her interest in photography fit nicely with her general view of things. She was sensitive to the natural world, and even at her age becoming what a later time would term an environmentalist. Of course, that word would have meant nothing to her, but what it signified fit her admirably.

Danny and John didn't share her enthusiasm for wildflowers, but they understood Mary saw the same thing in wildflowers – beauty – that they saw in the trout of the beaver ponds.

When the sun slipped below the tall ponderosas on the ridge to the west, the trout stopped feeding.

"Let's call it a day, Danny. I've never seen such crazy fishing."

"Me, either!" said Danny. "I think I caught a hundred!"

"I seriously doubt it."

"Well, I caught at least twenty."

The boys took their rods apart and stashed their gear in Frances. They knew porcupines relished the salty cork grips on fishing rods carelessly left out at night. Next, they scoured the woods for fallen limbs to use for firewood. John started their fire with a tepee of twigs, moving on to a log cabin of larger sticks. Once the fire burned down to a bed of coals, Mary began working up the meal by making pan bread. Louise had prepared biscuit mix for the kids to take on their trip by blending flour and other ingredients in a plastic bag. Now, beside the campfire, Mary added water to the bag and stirred it until it became a smooth, thick batter. She heated the cast iron skillet, and when it was hot, she poured it in. Like a giant pancake, the batter gradually puffed up and rose in the skillet. When the bottom looked nice and brown, she deftly flipped the bread in the air and it landed in the pan with the browned side up. After several minutes cooking the other side, she slid it out of the skillet onto a plate beside the fire and covered it with another plate to keep it warm. The bread smelled delicious.

Then John took over. For supper they'd brought ground beef and a can of baked beans. He browned the beef and seasoned it in the same skillet, and when done, he emptied the beans into the skillet and stirred them into the meat. Once this stew was bubbling hot, they spooned large helpings onto their tin plates. Each of the kids broke off a big chunk of the pan bread to use as a pusher. Using their pushers, they devoured the Hunter's Stew. The three washed the meal down with large cups of hot chocolate Danny brewed in their coffee pot. They all agreed that food couldn't taste any better than this.

After washing the supper dishes, they sat by their campfire talking and laughing. For Danny, seeing his brother and sister across the fire was so beautiful. The firelight danced and played on their features, producing an endless kaleidoscopic change of patterns and textures.

The protocol of campfire talk required that John initiate a topic upon which Mary would embroider. Then it would be Danny's turn. He strove to say interesting and important things but found it hard to keep up with the older kids. For their part, though, John and Mary gently coaxed Danny along, encouraging his insights.

"Wouldn't it be cool if we owned this land? We could build a cabin and live here for the summer," offered John. "I'd be a writer, and I'd have my window look out over the beaver dam. Come morning or evening, I could see the fish rising, and at night I'd watch the moonrise reflected on the surface of the pond. I'll bet that would inspire me to write great poems. I'd be like Thoreau living at Walden Pond."

"I'd put out a garden," Mary responded, "and grow tomatoes and nine rows of beans." She hoped she could sneak this allusion past John, but he caught it.

"So, would you have Yeats come out and help you pull weeds?" It was his role to be the family *literatus*, but he didn't speak sharply. It pleased him that Mary had read Yeats' poems and that she remembered this image from "The Lake Isle of Innisfree."

"We studied Ireland in our world history class," she explained. "We read some Irish poetry, and his were my favorites."

Danny was in over his head during this exchange, but, if nothing else, he was game.

"Beans would be good, and you could also plant corn; then we could make succotash."

John and Mary laughed, and when Danny realized they'd enjoyed his comment, he laughed as well.

"We'd need to have a telescope in an observatory tower," John continued. "On clear nights we could star gaze. Look up right now, over that tall spruce. You can see the Summer Triangle. It's made up of three great stars: Altair, Deneb, and Vega."

"Did you know the light we see coming from them is millions of years old? We're seeing them as they were millions of years ago," said Mary. "Maybe they don't even exist right now."

This concept astonished Danny. Could this be? Could the vast world out there be long since vanished? He couldn't think of a thing to say.

By now, with the firewood nearly gone, Danny put an amen to the evening. "Johnny and Mary, this was the *best* day! Thanks for letting me come with you."

The moon rose over the ridgeline and bathed the meadow and the woods in silver light. The three felt as if they were alone in the world with only their campfire, the night wind, and the purling creek. With the fire extinguished, and the night air so cold, the kids crawled into their bedrolls. Danny lay between Mary and John, and they all snuggled closely.

John unfolded two army blankets and pulled them over the three bedrolls. When the Milky Way rose above the eastern horizon, Danny imagined the Earth to be a basket with the Milky Way its starry handle. Just before he fell asleep, he thought about heaven. It was supposed to be a perfect place. He wondered how any place could be more perfect than this.

The morning dawned bright and clear. Danny awakened to the piping of a hermit thrush, the Pan of the forest. The grass around their camp glistened with frost, so when Danny walked down to the stream for water, frost crystals from the streamside willows fluttered down on him like snowflakes. Soon, the insects along the stream would become active in the warming sunlight, and the fish would begin feeding. He paused for a moment beside the placid pond, picked up a flat creek stone, and threw it as hard as he could. It skipped across the pond, making small splashes in a long curving path to the other bank. There would be no fishing this morning. He and John pestered the trout enough yesterday. Today, they'd let them feed in peace.

The kids struck their camp about ten and packed their gear into Frances for the trip home. Afterward, they policed the camp, picking up anything that would show people had camped there. Finally, they threw the fire ring stones into the woods and scattered the ashes.

Inside Frances, John and Mary sat in the two front seats. Using the bedrolls as cushions, Danny made a kind of lounge on top of the gear, and he sat there like a sultan surveying his domain. John and Mary occupied themselves by singing, salting their vocals with appropriate doo wops and finger snapping. They began with "Mr. Sandman," imitating the harmony of the Chordettes, then "Blueberry Hill" and "Heartbreak Hotel."

Next, Danny, wishing to make his own contribution to the medley, launched into a solo rendition of "Cielito Lindo," a song Luis Valdez had taught him. He sang with gusto in his best Mexican accent, trilling his *r*s:

> "Ay, ay, ay, ay,
> Canta y no llores,
> Porque cantando se alegran,
> Cielito Lindo, los corazones."

When he finished singing, John and Mary applauded. Delighted both with his performance and the big kids' approval, Danny blushed and bowed from atop his throne of bedrolls.

John smiled at Mary, "Hey, Danny, that's great. Mary and I know a little bit more of that song." Using the same melody, they sang the chorus of a racy campfire song.

"Ay, yi, yi, yi,
In China they never eat chili,
So sing me another verse
That's worse than the other verse,
And waltz me around again, Willy!"

They interspersed this refrain with limericks. However, they knew only a few G-rated limericks, so they gave up shortly and moved on to "Ninety-nine Bottles of Beer."

"Ninety-nine bottles of beer on the wall,
Ninety-nine bottles of beer,
Take one down and pass it around,
Ninety-eight bottles of beer."

When thirty bottles of beer had been taken down, Danny dropped out of the sing-along, enthralled by the mountains passing by his window. The domes and cliffs sloped steeply toward the canyon bottom leaving only room for the road, an old mining railroad, and Fountain Creek. Huge ponderosa pines stood along the road like sentinels and cast long shadows on the cascades and plunge pools of the creek as it rushed along. Danny was enchanted. The mountains were his heart country. He was coming to understand how profoundly they shaped his life. He couldn't imagine living anywhere else.

SIX

ICE ON THE SPRING POOL

But the days grow short when you reach September
When the autumn weather turns the leaves to flame
And one hasn't got time for the waiting game.
~ Maxwell Anderson ~

September always found Danny both happy and sad. His birthday this year fell on Labor Day, which made for a happy final summer weekend. Then, sadly, summer faded away, and the time came to go back to school. He was starting the eighth grade. Mary and John were, respectively, a sophomore and a senior in St. Mary's High School.

By the middle of September, the cottonwoods in the creeks and aspens on the mountainsides were a glorious yellow-gold in contrast to the cloudless blue sky. By late September, one could see the year drawing to a close, the days becoming crisp, the sunsets earlier, and the nights longer. By the beginning of October, the season's first snow frosted the summit of Pikes Peak. Winter would soon be upon them.

One afternoon in early November, after the kids arrived home from school, Danny rambled down the familiar path to visit Fred. In only a couple of minutes, he came running into the kitchen out of breath.

"You guys," he exclaimed, "There's ice on Fred's pool!"

Immediately, the kids ran down the path to the spring pool. At first, it was hard to tell, but when they looked closely, they could see a thin sheet of ice over its entire surface. The ice was very fragile, and John broke it up, pushing the pieces up onto the grassy pond edge. How, they wondered, would they feed Fred after the ice became thicker?

"We'd better ask Dad," said John solemnly. "He'll know what to do."

Russell sat reading the *Gazette-Telegraph* when the three burst into the kitchen. They all talked at once, describing Fred's predicament. How could they feed him when the ice grew thick? Russell folded the paper and sipped slowly from his cup of coffee.

"It's more serious than that, kids. When winter really arrives, the pool will freeze solid, and Fred will die."

"No!" cried Danny. "We can't just let him die. Isn't there something we can do to save him?"

"The only thing you can do is transfer him into deeper water where he can survive the winter."

"Can we put him in the lake?' asked Danny.

Russell shook his head slowly from side to side. "He might make it through the winter there, but in the summer the lake water is too warm, and he wouldn't survive. You'll need to find a place where the water is deep enough not to freeze solid, and where it will always be cold. Trout are cold water fish."

That night, Danny tossed restlessly for a while before going to sleep. How could he save Fred? What was the use of saving Fred from the restaurant kitchen only to lose him to the winter cold? By morning, he had a plan. Maybe it came to him in a dream. He couldn't tell, but he *was* sure it was a great plan. He dressed quickly and ran to the kitchen where the family sat eating breakfast.

"I know what we can do with Fred!" he blurted out. "Let's take him up to the beaver pond on Rule Creek. That will be a perfect place for him. He'll survive the winter, and when summer comes, he'll be happy with all the other trout."

"That's a pretty good idea," said Louise. "But how will you get him there?"

John spoke up. "We can carry him in a pail just like Danny did last spring. We'll drive there in Frances."

"The only problem I can see," said Russell, "is that he might not make it all the way to Rule Creek. Fish need oxygen, which they get out of the water they swim in. In the several hours it takes to drive there, Fred will probably run out of oxygen."

"I know!" said Mary. "We can take our bike tire pump with us. We'll stick the hose into the pail and pump air into the water to give Fred the oxygen he needs." She said the word *oxygen* with great authority. At school, she'd learned about the gases of Earth's atmosphere.

"Splendid," said their dad. "Your setup will be pretty primitive, but I think it just might work."

That settled the matter. It would surely be a dicey undertaking, because there had been a recent storm, and it would be snowy and cold in the mountains. As a result, the idea troubled Louise. The mountains north of Divide were still wild. The whole Lost Creek country northwest of Rule Creek remained a virtual wilderness. Every winter, people died from exposure in the mountains when they made mistakes or did careless things

When Louise and Russell were lying in bed on Friday night, she raised her concern. They often talked in the dark before falling asleep. The intimacy and privacy there allowed them to discuss things that couldn't be brought up at the supper table.

"Do you think this is a good idea, Russ? After all, it's just a fish that's causing all this commotion. I may seem insensitive, but in my mind, risking our kids' lives for a trout seems foolish."

"It's a hard thing to judge," Russell answered quietly. "We can't treat them like young children or they'll never gain self-confidence. We have to let them take risks. For us, the critical thing is weighing whether the risks are warranted or not. When I was seven, I taught myself to swim in the Gunnison River. At ten, I hunted and fished to help my mom put food on our table. I learned to fly at seventeen. I lived in hobo camps for two years before I was old enough to vote. I'm not bragging. I spent a lot of time lonely and frightened, and many terrible things happened to me. But they made me what I am.

"I wouldn't want our kids to go through what I did, but, on the other hand, I want them to be tough and self-reliant. There are no shortcuts to those virtues. The secret is balance; we have to balance the risks against the rewards. In this case, I don't think the risks are too great. If they're not home by supper, I know where they're going, and I could get to them in an hour and a half."

"I know, I know," whispered Louise. "You're right."

Although very different from his, her early years were hard in other ways. Louise had an urban upbringing, the baby of seven, her mother having died when Louise was six years old. During grade school, she kept house for her family. All her clothes were hand-me-downs. Her two older brothers and four older sisters worked, and they expected supper would be ready when they came home.

She worked all through high school, riding the streetcars around Denver by herself. On almost every payday, her father went on a bender. When he finally came home, Louise would undress him, clean him up, and put him to bed. The next morning, it would be her job to pack his lunch bucket and get him off to the railroad yard before she went to school. In many ways, she didn't have a girlhood. She understood intimately the meaning of fear and loneliness.

Russell reached out in the dark and touched her arm. She turned over against him and kissed him tenderly. "I just worry."

———◆———

After making preparations on Saturday morning, the kids were off to Rule Creek with John driving Frances, Fred in a pail of water, Danny furiously pumping air into the pail, and Mary supervising. Highway 24 climbed steadily up Ute Pass all the way to Divide, nearly thirty miles. Frances was powered by a four-cylinder engine designed before World War II and made to haul soldiers across a rugged battlefield, but not made for speed. Thus, the jeep labored along at forty miles an hour.

"Can't we go any faster?" Danny asked anxiously.

"Be patient, Danny. We'll get there soon enough."

Danny was concerned because of his dad's warning about the oxygen

Mallalrd Ducks
Anas platyrhynchos

Mallard Drake and Hen Poised for Flight

in the pail. But, at the rate he pumped, there would be enough oxygen for Fred to survive for a year.

When they reached Woodland Park, Mary passed around peanut butter sandwiches their mom had prepared for them. She'd also packed potato chips and a bottle of pop for each of the kids. Mary busily pried off the bottle caps and passed the lunches around. Danny wolfed his down and resumed his frantic pumping.

The rusty coffee can still perched on the stump, marking the entrance to the secret road. John turned Frances into the aspens and began the slow crawl along the rutted trail toward Rule Creek. How different the landscape now appeared in contrast to their first trip in August. The aspens were bare of leaves and stood along the trail like gaunt sculptures. Winter had already come to the mountains. Snow drifts lay across the trail, remnants of the recent storm. John needed to take care not to get Frances stuck in the snow. It would be a long walk out for help.

Since the trail drifted steadily downhill, Frances punched through the snow without much difficulty. However, the return trip would be more difficult, when the little jeep would have to break through the drifts on an uphill slope.

"I sure hope we can get back up this trail," John said to Mary, the worry obvious in his voice.

When at last they emerged from the trees into the valley, a very different scene greeted them. The wildflowers were gone, and the meadow grass was brown and dead. Large snow patches were scattered across the meadow. The pond had ice over most of its surface, but some open water beckoned at the point where the inlet stream entered. The stream wasn't frozen because moving water is difficult to freeze.

A pair of mallards, a drake and a hen, flushed off the open water with a racket of wings and quacks. They swung over the meadow and flashed down the valley in the pale afternoon sunlight. The kids were surprised and thrilled by the beautiful vignette.

Then they turned to the task of saving Fred. "We can put him into the inlet stream, and he'll go from there right into the pond," said John.

"Won't he die here just like in the frozen spring pool?" asked Danny.

"No. He'll be fine," Mary countered. "This pond is way too deep to freeze solid. Fred and his new trout friends will be safe through the winter, because the creek will stay open. He'll have plenty of oxygen."

John took the pail and carefully tiptoed over the frozen marsh to the edge of the inlet stream. Mary and Danny were right behind him and watched over his shoulder as he delicately shooed the fish out of the pail into the creek. Fred slipped into the water, got himself aligned with the current, and tried to swim upstream. John quickly got him turned around, whereupon he shot down the creek, slipped under the icy lid and into the dark pond. The three stood for a moment in silence. They were happy to have given Fred a chance at a new life, but sad to see their friend disappear from their lives.

John broke the silence. "Don't worry, Danny. Fred will be fine here. Although we can't see him, we know he's in the pond just being a trout and probably loving it. Come on. Let's go home. I just hope Frances can get us out of here."

Danny stood looking at the dark water for a moment. "*Adiós*, Fred," he said quietly, "*Adiós*."

———⋅◈⋅———

The drive out of the valley was harrowing. Each of the snow drifts had melted some in the midday sunlight, so a muddy patch lay before each one. John approached the first drift slowly and carefully. Immediately, Frances began to spin her tires. John stopped and backed up.

"Hang on, you guys! We're going on Mr. Toad's Wild Ride!"

He pressed the gas pedal to the floorboard, and the jeep leaped forward. When Frances hit the mud and the snow drift, she bumped and jumped, slipped and slid, but in the end she made it through. Mary and Danny were amazed, frightened, and thrilled. They conquered drift after drift in the same way leading to the final one, the longest and deepest across the trail right before it reached the level woods atop the ridge.

"This is it," John said with determination. "Hang on!"

He backed up about twenty yards to make a run at the snow. Then he rushed at the big drift with the engine whining, Mary and Danny yelling encouragement. Frances slammed into the snow, lurched and bucked, spun, slipped, and came to a halt. John didn't waste a second. He shifted quickly into reverse, and Frances plunged backwards and out of the drift.

"What are we going to do now?" asked Mary. "Frances can't make it through."

John thought for a moment.

"Okay, let's help her a little bit."

The three kids fanned out through the woods searching for rocks and sticks. They threw all the stuff they gathered into the snow where Frances had faltered. John hoped these things would give her more traction in order to get past this spot. The kids piled back into the jeep and waited to see if Frances could best the snow. Once again, John backed up. This time he backed up to the very edge of the previous snow drift. This would give him the longest run possible before he hit the snow.

"Here we go!" he shouted.

"Come on, Frances!" urged Mary and Danny.

The jeep careened toward the big drift, smashed into it, plunged forward, on, on, into the bad spot, slipped, grabbed, bucked, grabbed, and then out.

———✦———

Night descended quickly after sunset, and the cold mountain air chilled them as they chugged down Ute Pass. The heater whirred nosily making a valiant effort to keep up with the cold but was gradually losing. John kept a couple of army blankets in the back of the jeep for times like this. The kids all wrapped themselves up. John and Mary chatted happily until the lights of town appeared in the distance.

Danny, however, fell into a thoughtful silence, overwhelmed by the variety and intensity of the day's emotions. There'd been the joyful euphoria when he came up with the plan to save Fred, but he'd been anxious all through the long drive up Ute Pass, concerned Fred would not survive the trip. Then again, the sudden flush of the wild ducks, their sleekness and the colors of their plumage, had thrilled him. Finally, just at sundown, he watched sadly as his trout darted under the icy lid of the beaver pond. Now, on the ride home, turning these images over and over in his mind, he felt emotionally drained.

Sensing his younger brother's feelings, John said, "Danny, I read a fine poem in English class last week. It's called, 'Ode to the West Wind.' The last few lines are really beautiful. Listen to this,

> 'Scatter, as from an unextinguished hearth,
> Ashes and sparks, my words among mankind!
> Be through my lips to unawakened Earth
> The trumpet of a prophecy! O Wind,
> If Winter comes, can Spring be far behind?'

He's saying winter will pass, and spring will awaken things. It means when all seems to be going badly, it will get better soon."

Danny thought about these words. He understood what they meant, that life is a mixture of joy and sadness. After this sad winter day and saying goodbye to Fred, spring days, brighter days, would eventually come. Growing up, he now understood, would be both unhappy and joyful by turns. He would have to accept that Fred would no longer frolic in the spring pool behind their home. Fred the Trout had moved out of Danny's life and into a new one in the mountains. The happy trips down the path across the rattlesnake glade were a thing of the past.

Danny's splendid summer, he realized, was written and now part of his personal story, not to be lived again. He saw that life takes many unexpected turns, and one never knows what lies in store.

SEVEN

TERROR IN THE SKY

Off we go into the wild blue yonder,
Keep the wings level and true;
If you'd live to be a gray-haired wonder
Keep the nose out of the blue.
— Robert M. Crawford —

On several occasions during the summer, Russell took the family flying. For example, one Sunday after Mass, they flew to Denver. Louise's sister and her husband met the Grays and took them out for breakfast. These junkets reinforced Russell's oft repeated point that private aircraft are eminently safe, safer in fact than automobiles. But among experienced pilots, the insider joke described flying as hours of incredible boredom interspersed with moments of stark terror. John and Danny were to discover the wisdom hidden behind the façade of humor.

In late November, Russell arranged to take the boys out of school for the last two days of the week. This wasn't unusual. Parents took their children out of school for all manner of reasons deemed important. St. Mary's was small enough that the nuns knew the school families well, and they were tolerant of such occasions when the request seemed reasonable. In this particular instance, Russell planned to go pheasant hunting in South Dakota, and he thought John was old enough to hunt and Danny would profit by the experience. Ed Bartlett, who had helped John to refurbish his jeep, would complete the foursome. Ed was a seasoned hunter and a fine wing shot. Raised on a farm in the lower Arkansas valley, he'd hunted all his life.

The Thursday departure went smoothly. Since Russell planned to be underway shortly after daybreak, he awakened the boys in the predawn darkness. Louise prepared a breakfast for the family. Mary busied herself helping both her mom and the men where she could. She had no interest in hunting, and Louise planned a shopping expedition to make up for her exclusion.

When the hunters reached Peterson Field, the boys eagerly helped load the gear into the red and white Cessna. After the practiced rhythm of gassing up and the preflight check, Russell taxied the plane out to the runway, and when cleared for takeoff by the tower, the pheasant hunters were soon airborne and South Dakota bound.

The weather was classically autumnal, with a cloudless blue sky that stretched from horizon to horizon. Having climbed to his cruising altitude, Russell picked up the Omni radio beacon, and the little plane bored into the sunrise.

"Ed, you and the boys are not going to believe the number of birds up there in the dry lakes west of Watertown. The locals are calling these last several seasons the 'Glory Years.' I've hunted pheasants in eastern Colorado and western Kansas for many years, and I've never seen anything like the number of birds in South Dakota."

"Well, I'll tell you what," Ed responded, "I can't wait to see it. From what I've heard, it's a spectacle."

"Won't we have our limits in just a few minutes?" asked John. "It won't be much fun to leave the fields at nine in the morning. What'll we do in Watertown for the rest of the day?"

"To begin," Russell answered, "the hunt doesn't open until noon. That means we'll sleep in, have a leisurely breakfast, and then drive out to the farm where we're going to hunt. We'll get there in time for the noon start. As for limiting out, I'm not going to say much."

When Russell finished, he turned and grinned at Ed, who sat in the co-pilot's seat.

Both men knew how unnerving the flush of a half-dozen pheasants can be. All the pandemonium coming from underfoot – the roar of their wings, the frantic cackling – can literally paralyze a hunter. The tendency is to empty one's shotgun in the general direction of the departing birds, usually without so much as pulling a feather. The problem isn't the lack of targets, it's the difficulty of controlling one's reactions and remaining calm. To make matters worse, only the roosters can be legally killed. Amid the chaos of the flush, the hunter has to distinguish the roosters from the hens, because shooting hens is a serious offense, and what is more, a shameful thing. The ultimate scorn one pheasant hunter can heap upon another is to call him a hen shooter.

A few hours more of such conversation while winging over the far-reaching sand hills of Nebraska and the South Dakota prairie brought the hunters to Watertown and an uneventful landing. They settled into the local hotel, the boys in one room, Russell and Ed in another. After supper at the Tall Corn Café, the four passed the evening in animated conversation about hunting, flying, and life in general. It was a rich soup for Danny who soaked up the language, the ideas, and the sheer manliness of the talk like a sponge.

———◆———

The first day's hunt went just as expected. The birds boiled out of the cattail marshes in swarms ahead of the hunters. After getting over his initial shock, John got used to the explosive flush of pheasant roosters and made several fine shots. Russell and Ed, predictably, limited out quickly. In one memorable scene, Danny and John watched from atop a hill as their dad hunted out a small weedy thicket several hundred yards away. To their amazement, he flushed three roosters, two of which flew straight away, with the third swinging around and fleeing in the opposite direction. He dropped the first two birds with two shots, and then turned and killed the third with a shot that pressed forty-five yards. The boys were awestruck.

The second and final day repeated the first except for one very unusual incident. The four were hunting through a harvested cornfield where a windbreak of Osage orange trees edged the field. At one point, Russell crossed the fence and went through the trees into the adjacent field in order to hunt out a promising small patch of standing corn. Unseen by him, another hunting party appeared at the end of the first field preparing to launch their own hunt. They were probably three hundred yards away. This complicated the situation, because, as the two parties drew closer, careless shots might injure a hunter. Russell couldn't see these hunters, and when he flushed a rooster from the little patch of corn, his shot sprinkled lead pellets on them. Nothing truly dangerous occurred. The lead pellets fell out of the sky at a steep angle and were more annoying than dangerous. Nonetheless, his shot violated hunting decorum. In a few minutes, the two parties came together, and one man strode up menacingly and began berating Russell and Ed. Russell responded by suggesting the wayward shot came from a different hunting party in the adjacent field, and with this massaging of the truth, the crisis passed.

Danny and John were dumbstruck. They saw their dad take his shot and drop the bird. They knew it was he who had rained the shot pellets on the other hunters. Both boys were chagrined and embarrassed by their dad's calmly offered diplomatic lie. Russell immediately realized he'd deeply disappointed his sons, but he didn't know what to say, and so he said nothing. Ed, for his part, didn't care. In his view, Russell had done the correct thing. It would have been foolish and unproductive to engage the other hunters in a shouting match. Let sleeping dogs lie.

The trip home the next day began without ceremony. In the minds of the two boys, the wayward shot incident loomed like a storm cloud. Such was the measure of respect they held for their father that, to them, it seemed inconceivable he could lie with such seeming ease. Thus, as the four flew homeward, Ed carried the burden of conversation with Russell responding just often enough to give the impression of interest and the boys maintaining a petulant silence in the rear seats.

For several hours, the plane buzzed along on a west southwest course. As a matter of customary practice, Russell flew by visual reference whenever possible, and his favorite method was to pick up a principal railroad or highway and follow it. Presently, he switched from one wing tank to the other.

"We didn't get very far on that tank of gas did we, Russell?" Ed asked in his typically dry manner.

"Not as far as I planned." Concern edged his voice. "We're flying into a big cyclone, and we're bucking really strong headwinds. Out here the prevailing winds are westerly, and today, they're really blowing. We're not making the ground speed I hoped we would. To complicate matters," he continued, "the gas guy at Watertown didn't fill this tank completely full. Shame on me. I should've checked more carefully."

By now, they were at 9,500 ft. winging over the golden plains of northern Nebraska. As far as one could see from the plane, there was only the endless prairie overlain with a filigree of coulees and dry creeks. Sandstone bluffs occasionally broke the visual monotony.

"I hoped to reach Scottsbluff for gas and lunch," Russell said quietly, half to himself. "It should have been easy to make it there, but now, we won't come close."

The sparse population of these prairies presented a problem. Western Nebraska is a vast expanse of badlands and timbered creeks. The few tiny towns on Russell's chart didn't have landing strips much less airports, the lone exception being Chadron. On the chart it showed the landing strip there was radio controlled, so that became their new destination. It would be well short of Scottsbluff, but it should be doable.

Danny sensed the concern in the conversation between Russell and Ed. Ed was also a licensed pilot but had far less experience than Russell.

"Are we okay, Dad?" he asked, fear verging on panic beginning to churn his stomach.

Russell's Cessna 170

John leaped into the breach, as much to reassure himself as to calm Danny. "Don't worry. Dad and Ed can definitely handle this. Look at the gas gauge. There's still some left."

Each wing tank had its own gauge. The right tank showed empty, with the left tank now getting dangerously low. John grew increasingly fearful himself, but he didn't want to show that to his brother.

"Chadron is only twenty miles," Russell said. He turned around and smiled at his two sons. "It's only a few minutes until we land and have lunch. Are you boys up for that?"

Russell wasn't overly concerned. He had considerable experience with primitive and difficult flying conditions. When he'd learned to fly at seventeen, he toured his dilapidated Jenny around western Colorado and eastern Utah, landing on dirt roads, even occasionally in pastures. Now, twenty-five years later, he had thousands of hours on his license, and many of those hours were logged under less than ideal conditions.

At this point, Russell tried to raise the radio at the Chadron airstrip. Giving his call sign and location, he asked for landing permission and instructions. The radio crackled immediately:

"Cessna N3152X, you can't land here. We're experiencing strong ground winds with occasional gusts to 50 mph. Fly on to Scottsbluff.

Russell keyed the mike; "I'm either going to land at Chadron or crash. We're out of gas. I repeat, we're out of gas."

"So be it, Cessna, it's up to you. You pays your money, you takes your choice," responded the radioman with droll humor.

"Chadron, do you have a gas truck?"

"Yes, we do," the radio shot back.

"Are there a few guys around the hangar?"

"Yeah, there are a couple of mechanics, probably four or five guys altogether."

"Have them come out to the runway. When I get this airplane on the ground, have several of them grab the tail and a couple on each wing. Then bring up the truck and gas me up as fast as possible."

"Roger. We will help you as much as we can. For God's sake, be careful!"

By this time, they could see the single slender runway. Fortunately, it was aligned almost perfectly with the wind so Russell wouldn't be making a crosswind landing. Instead of the typical gradual loss of altitude and gentle angle of approach, he held the plane two hundred feet off the ground and throttled back. The wind buffeted the plane like a leaf. When they were a quarter of a mile from the knot of men standing beside the runway, he began his descent. He alternately applied flaps, then throttle, then flaps, then throttle. Each time he did this the stall horn blared. Both boys were terrified. Danny began to cry. John wrapped his arm around his brother and pulled him close.

Down, down, down went the plane. Just when it seemed they would touch the ground, a gust of wind would pick the plane up, and Russell would struggle for control. Suddenly, the plane touched the ground, not twenty yards from the men and the gas truck.

While Russell fought to keep control, the men did as he'd asked and anchored the plane. Immediately, the gas truck filled the tanks, and then pulled clear. Through his open window, Russell handed the nearest man a hundred-dollar bill. There was no time to worry about change. The airport crew had earned the remainder as a tip.

Russell yelled against the wind. "When I give you the high sign, everyone let her go."

He neutralized the controls, checked his instruments, and pushed in the throttle. With the engine roaring, he waved out the window, and the men holding the plane down all let go and jumped clear. The wind grabbed the little Cessna, and it was instantly airborne. Russell fought to control it, keeping it facing into the wind. The plane shot skyward, and the Chadron airport receded into the distance.

"In all my flying, I have never seen anything like that," Ed said, amazement akin to reverence in his voice. "That was the damnedest thing. I figured we were goners."

Russell sat silently for a moment. Then he turned to face his sons. "I'm proud of you boys. Someday you will tell your kids about our wild ride. Danny, don't be ashamed of crying. Being thrown around by the wind, with the stall horn barking, I was on the verge of tears myself."

Ed laughed. "Believe me, so was I."

Danny curled up in his seat, pretending to sleep. On the one hand, he'd heard his dad tell a bald-faced lie, a thing Danny thought to be sinful and unmanly. Yet, he'd just witnessed a feat of extraordinary courage and skill. His dad seemed like one of the heroes in the books he'd read. It presented a paradox too difficult for Danny to fathom.

By the time they reached Petersen Field several hours later, the weather had changed completely, and they landed smoothly and uneventfully. The unloading of the plane and the drive home passed without much talk. On several occasions, Russell tried to start a conversation with his sons, but both John and Danny were quiet, staring absently out the windows of the car. When they turned into their driveway off Elm Circle, Louise and Mary came out to greet the mighty hunters. The sounds and smells of home and supper warmed the boys' hearts, and soon they were recounting the excitement of the hunt and the terror of the flight across Nebraska.

Louise clucked her tongue and upbraided Russell. "I thought flying was safer than driving," she chided.

"Oh, Sweetheart, the boys are exaggerating. It wasn't too bad."

Danny glanced at John to see his reaction.

John spoke up immediately. "It scared me some, Mom, but Dad had everything under control. I never doubted for a minute we were safe."

Now, John was lying like a rug. Danny remembered the terrified look on John's face when the plane lunged and swayed with the stall horn blaring. People lie, he saw, for many reasons. His dad lied about his wayward shot in order to avoid a confrontation. John lied to provide support for his dad's account of their flight. It was confusing.

Later that night, when the boys were chatting in their beds before falling asleep, Danny raised this moral dilemma.

"I don't get it. Dad lied in the cornfield about taking a shot, and you lied at supper tonight about the plane ride. I thought lying is a sin."

John thought for a moment.

"There are a couple of things, Danny. First, just because something is wrong doesn't make it a sin. If a man steals food to feed his starving children, it's not a sin. On the other hand, if a man tells the truth in order to hurt someone, he has sinned. The important thing is what you intend. If you intend to do good, that's the important thing, no matter what you actually do. Thomas Aquinas said sin is in the will, not in the deed.

"The other thing is to remember even great men have weak moments. Look how St. Peter denied three times he knew Jesus. The ancient Greeks called this *hubris*. Father Stevins explained this to us in religion class a couple of weeks ago. No human being is completely perfect. Everyone has weaknesses. He read us a passage from Scripture that says even the just man falls seven times daily. I know you're bothered by catching Dad in a lie; it really hurt me, too. But think about it. Dad is a war hero, he is a great father, he is loved by nearly everyone. I could go on and on. I think you and I are demanding too much of him."

John lay silent after this ethical meditation. Lying in the darkness, Danny smiled. He realized he was being unfair to his dad. The lie was such a small thing. His dad had lied because he hadn't wanted a huge argument with a loud-mouthed stranger over something trivial. What about his landing the plane at Chadron? That was almost a miracle. Didn't that mean anything? Russell had accomplished what very few men would have the courage or skill to do.

"All right," he said to himself, "It's okay," and then fell asleep.

EIGHT

SNOW BUCKING

Over the harvest-fields forsaken,
Silent, and soft, and slow
Descends the snow.
~ William W. Longfellow ~

In 1956, the ability of city crews to remove snow was primitive, relying on a few trucks with plows. The state was more professional, if that is the right word, and its plows were big four-wheel drive International Harvester trucks with chains on all the tires. At best, however, their ability to manage large snowfalls remained marginal.

When the kids went to bed on a Tuesday night, KRDO forecast a heavy snowfall over the next several days, nothing unusual for Colorado Springs in December. However, all the announcements had an ominous tone with the forecast couched in vague terms as to amounts of snow and wind conditions. This had all the earmarks of no school today.

By eight on Wednesday morning, the view out the living room window toward the mountains showed a whiteout, snow falling in flakes as large as quarters. Visibility shrank to no more than a few yards, and what could be seen looked like a white desert. To call the kids' mood festive would be a gross understatement. There are few childhood ecstasies more profound than school cancellation due to snow.

"No school today," crowed Danny. "They just announced on KRDO that St. Mary's is closed."

"Look at it fall," seconded John. "At this rate we might luck out and not have class until Monday."

Mary wasn't happy. She loved school, and today she was scheduled to read the poems she'd composed on the theme of winter. Proud of her composition, Mary looked forward to plaudits from Sister Mary John. This turn of events would postpone for an indefinite time her starring in the class.

<hr />

The previous night at supper she'd rehearsed her performance for the family. Standing up in her place at the table, she first looked furtively at John to see if he were paying attention.

"'The Snowfall' by Mary Gray," she began, with more than a touch of drama,

> "Look! How fast the snow is falling,
> Perhaps it's Nature's way of calling,
> Calling us to look and see
> How beautiful the world can be.
>
> But time will melt it all away,
> And blue skies will replace the gray.
> With us just as with the snow,
> We come into the world then go.
>
> The winter earth is brown again
> As if the snow had never been.
> Where has it gone, the vanished snow?
> Where am I going? I don't know."

When Mary finished, she made a courtly bow and everyone clapped.

"Mary, that was just lovely!" her mom exulted, dabbing her eyes with her napkin. "I could almost feel the snowflakes landing on my face and hands. You have your father's gift with words. You know it's true, Russ, she does. It's a fine thing."

"I agree with Mom," Russell continued. "It's beautiful, Sweetheart. I love the way you raise a big question at the end that grows naturally out of your snow images. Beautiful!"

The kids were confident of their parents' love, and when Louise and Russell singled one of them out, the other two always enjoyed the moment vicariously. John and Danny had both chimed in.

"¡*Su poema es muy hermosa*! It should be a song. I bet I could sing it right now," Danny enthused, beaming at his own literary flourish.

To add his bit of erudite commentary, John, ever the scholar, observed, "I learned in Latin class that the ancient Romans used the same word for a poem and a song – *carmen*. To them, all poems were musical, and all songs were poetical."

Mary blushed and looked down shyly at the paper in her hand. Her family's praise always pleased her.

Mary's poem was prescient. The snow piled up at an amazing rate. Already, there were six inches on the little yews in front of the porch, and the storm had just begun. After breakfast, the family gathered in front of the picture window in the living room watching the falling snow, seeing just "how beautiful the world can be."

By four, a foot of snow lay on the ground, with yet more coming. Throughout the morning and early afternoon, the kids exhausted themselves in all manner of snow diversions – sledding, snowball fights, chasing Junior through the deepening snow, around and around, they laughing and he adroitly dodging their attempts at capture.

By eight in the evening, matters were obviously getting serious. KRDO broadcast public service announcements constantly, advising people to stay in their homes and to avoid all but essential car trips. This latter admonition was pointless. The depth of the snow on the unplowed streets of town made car travel impossible except for those fortunate few who owned jeeps.

During the night, the snowfall diminished. Sixteen inches had fallen on Broadmoor, and conditions were markedly worse. The temperature plunged into the single digits, and the wind rose until it gusted to forty miles an hour. This was now a ground blizzard as the wind blew, whipped, and stacked up the fallen snow into drifts, some of which were many feet deep. The wind piled the snow in front of the Gray home all the way to the eaves of the roof. Whenever an obstacle opposed its movement, the wind piled up a barchan dune until the landscape seemed to be a snow desert strewn with unrecognizable debris.

By Thursday morning, the world of Mary's poem, so beautiful to see, had become savage and menacing. Anyone caught outside and unprotected would be in real danger. Many neighborhoods lost power because of lines taken down by broken trees. The Grays counted themselves fortunate since their home wasn't affected.

Colorado Springs had become an isolated enclave. The highways connecting it in all directions were closed by huge drifts of windblown snow. Peterson Field appeared abandoned and lifeless. The town itself became a collection of little knots of people barricaded in their homes. Many found a wall of snow confronting them when they opened their doors. No cars moved. The stoplights in town doggedly flashed red and green to empty streets.

KRDO fell upon an ingenious idea. In the town there were several dozen jeeps, most of whose owners belonged to the local jeep club. The station enlisted their aid in a scheme to deliver emergency services throughout the stricken region. Each jeep owner willing to participate received a number. People could then call the station with requests – a medical prescription badly needed, for instance – and the station would notify a jeep by number over the air, giving the appropriate instructions for the appointed errand of mercy. John immediately signed himself up and prepared number thirteen Frances for serious business. Of course, Mary and Danny immediately volunteered as yeomen in the project.

For much of the day, the chores were mundane – groceries, medicine, and such – delivered to grateful citizens. In some cases, the

Jeep Snow Bucking in a Blizzard

jeeps became an ersatz taxi service hauling doctors, policemen, and other essential people here and there. All this was gratis to the town, with the jeep owners buying their own gasoline, although most of those who were aided tipped generously. It was a Rube Goldberg arrangement, but it worked remarkably well.

By nightfall, around five, conditions worsened further. Now the blowing snow and darkness combined to limit visibility, and the relentless wind piled the snow into yet deeper drifts. Inside Frances, the kids tried to stay warm as they went from crisis to crisis. There were, of course, no CB radios much less cell phones. After each errand, John would have to find a telephone in order to call the station and report on his mission. To the jeeps scattered across El Paso County thrashing around in the deep snow, the AM radio amounted to a thin, one-way umbilical cord that connected them to the safe indoor world. Frances didn't have a radio, so the kids listened intently to Mary's portable radio for information and instructions.

When they reached home in the early evening, Russell suggested they call it a night.

"You kids have done much more than your duty. Maybe we should all play cards or watch TV. Tomorrow will bring more trials and triumphs."

Mary was still listening to her radio when it announced that jeep number thirteen needed to make an important run, and John should call the station for instructions.

"I'll see what they want," said John as he dialed the radio station's number. "We could make one more run tonight."

On the phone, John nodded occasionally and finally said, "All right" to someone on the other end of the line. When he hung up, he explained. "There isn't anyone else available, and this is really important. A woman who lives out on the prairie is going into labor. She needs to get to the hospital. We have to go right now."

The weather had become very dangerous. Russell was torn, reluctant to send his kids off into such a night.

"Russ, you go with the boys," said Louise, settling the matter as she often did. "Mary and I will mind the radio. There's an expectant mother out there who needs your help."

"Okay, boys, I'll go with you," Russell said after a brief, pensive silence. "Mom, if we're not back in three hours, call the radio station and have them send a couple of jeeps to help us."

The night had become a maelstrom of wind and snow. Several miles east of Peterson Field, they turned south onto the appointed section road. These roads were natural snow traps, with the wind stacking deep drifts between the two state fences that marked the edges of adjoining fields. Frances couldn't simply plow through the drifts, by now too deep and crusted by the wind. John had to buck the snow, lunging into a drift, then backing up, lunging again, and again, until the jeep broke through into a temporary respite between drifts.

John and his dad were quiet. For his part, Danny kept up a continuous monologue. At one point, Frances seemed about to bog down and stall in the deep snow.

"Come on, Johnny, you're doing great! Remember how Frances did at Rule Creek. She can do this!" Danny pled, half to encourage John and half to reassure himself.

Russell turned around and squeezed his son's knee. "Don't worry, Danny, John is a great driver. We'll be fine."

Immediately, his anxiety lessened. If his dad said all was well, it was.

Danny's comment had a different effect on John. His mind flashed back to Rule Creek only a month ago and the snow bucking he'd done there. How tame that now seemed in retrospect. Then, there were only a few hundred yards of trail to break in broad daylight. Now, they faced several miles of hellish snow bucking amid disorienting windblown snow, through a trackless waste, with virtually no visibility. The jaunty bravado of this morning had given way to creeping fear.

Only the faint glow of the instruments in the dash illumined the interior of the jeep. While Frances' engine whined and her four chained tires churned through the snow, John and his dad strained to make out the road ahead.

"What are those lights?" Russell exclaimed suddenly.

As if by magic, two beams of light piercing the night like search-lights came into view several hundred yards up the road. When Frances came abreast, they saw the cause. A state plow truck, enormous and powerful, lay on its side in the borrow pit where it had tumbled, and its headlights were pointing up at a 60° angle. The driver was unhurt, but his radio antenna hung limply, broken off by the plunge. The driver emerged from the stricken truck and waved them to a halt. John opened his door in order to talk to the driver, and explained to him the nature of their errand.

"Why don't you come with us," John offered. "We will eventually get you back to town."

Although another passenger would crowd the jeep, his additional weight would provide improved traction. The driver looked skeptically into Frances through the open door and politely declined. When he failed to check in by radio, he said, the another state crew would come looking for him.

"No, no, it seems to me you guys have your hands full," he shouted over the wind, obviously incredulous that the little jeep would fare better than his diesel-powered behemoth.

It seemed an eternity until a forlorn looking roadside mailbox appeared out of the swirling snow. Frances turned and plunged down the lane to the farmhouse, toward the welcome porch light, toward the windows showing lamps and curtains and expectant faces peering out into the snowy night.

John and Russell entered the warmth and light of the entry hall to assist the woman whose name was Marjorie.

"Call me Margie," she said. Her story was brief and compelling. She lived with her mother while her husband, a soldier, served overseas. With her complicated pregnancy, her doctor feared an attempt at homebirth, with only her mom to assist her, could prove disastrous.

Carefully, Russell escorted Margie to the jeep, supporting her gently. It was a delicate project getting her into the back seat, and once they were underway, Russell turned and spoke to her.

"Don't worry, Margie," he said. "We will get you to St. Francis Hospital before you know it. You and your baby will be fine."

Saying things will be fine was pure Russell. He was that sort of man, and he spent much of his life trying to make things fine for others. To keep her warm, Danny fetched an army blanket from behind the seat.

"You will be fine; my dad says so," he assured her, as he tucked the blanket behind her shoulders with self-conscious clumsiness.

The return to town proved a reprise of the journey out until something hulking and mechanical suddenly loomed out of the swirling snow. Since they passed this spot a half-hour earlier, a local farmer had tried to drive his grain truck to town, had bogged down and then abandoned it. John pounded the steering wheel with his fists.

"What are we going to do now? This guy has completely blocked the road."

"Take it easy, son," cautioned Russell. "There's just enough room to squeeze around him on the left. We have no choice. Do your best."

Danny leaned forward between the two front seats to see better what concerned John and Russell. "¡Dios mio!" he blurted out.

Russell climbed out of the jeep into the wind-driven snow, and, standing in the headlights, guided John carefully with hand signals. Frances edged gingerly alongside the big truck, but just when it seemed as though they'd made safe passage, the left rear tire dropped off the edge of the road, and the jeep foundered. All four tires thrashed with futility; they were stuck fast.

John climbed out of the jeep quickly and grabbed the come-along out of the foot well of the driver's seat. It used six feet of chain, and John had an additional fifty feet of steel cable. John came around to the front of Frances and hooked the come-along to her bumper. Then he struggled through the deep snow of the borrow pit to the state fence, where he hooked the cable around a stout fence post. Luckily, this post stood at a fence corner and was strongly supported. Having explained its operation to his dad, he mounted up in Frances once more. This was a difficult problem. Would the come-along pull Frances out of the snow, or would it pull down the fence post?

John beeped the horn to signal his dad to begin working the long ratchet handle back and forth while the jeep growled and dug at the snow. Link by link Russell pulled the chain through the ratchet, and inch by inch Frances crept forward. Once the stranded tire climbed out of the ditch, she could move again. Russell threw the come-along and cable into the footwell and climbed back into the jeep. He looked like a snowman with a rime of snow clinging to his coat and gloves, but he grinned happily and off they went.

Soon, the lights of town glowed dimly through the blowing snow. In a few minutes, they were at the entrance to the hospital. Aided by John and Russell, Margie climbed awkwardly down from the jeep, and while the emergency staff helped her into a wheelchair, she bid farewell to her rescuers.

"I shall never forget you all, never," she said, addressing the three Grays through her tears.

———◆———

Russell spoke quietly as the three worked their way south over the snow-choked streets toward home. "You boys did a fine thing tonight. I'm very proud of you."

"Thanks for coming with us, Dad." John answered. "I was scared to death. You made all the difference. We could never have done it without you."

In the back seat, Danny sat in silence. He was emotionally exhausted from the day's activities, capped off by the dramatic rescue of Margie from the clutches of the storm. The drama, the fear, and the exultation were almost too much for him to bear. Now safe and homeward bound, he wrapped himself in the army blanket and luxuriated in the privilege of just being in such company.

NINE

HUNTING GEESE WITH DAD

My Heart knows what the wild goose knows
And I must go where the wild goose goes.
Wild goose, brother goose, which is best?
A wandering foot, or a heart at rest?
~ Terry Gilkyson ~

The old Studebaker bumped along a farm road in the half-light just before daybreak one bitterly cold January morning. This was typically how goose hunts began. The rutted road lay packed with ice from several heavy snowfalls, and it challenged Russell as he drove east toward the dawn. There were no defrosters in the Studebaker, and all the windows had a film of frost. Russell continually rubbed off the windshield with his gloved hand, clearing a small circle of glass through which he could see the dimly lit road. Uncle Ed Brinson sat in the passenger seat sipping coffee from the cap of his thermos bottle.

Uncle Ed wasn't really the Gray kids' uncle. He and his wife, Aunt Rita, were longtime friends of Louise and Russell, and they easily settled into the role of uncle and aunt. A decade older than Russell, Uncle Ed served in the Navy during the Great War. He didn't hunt, but he often came along on these expeditions, because he relished the friendship and the outdoor life. His great love was fly fishing, which he did stylishly in a three-piece suit. For several summers, Uncle Ed had taken John on a fishing trip to the Lake Fork of the Gunnison

River. He presented a strange sight, standing in the river in hip boots, looking like a Victorian gentleman from a vintage English print.

In between sips of coffee, he coached Russell's driving. Russell often told the kids Uncle Ed was an old woman, and he bore Ed's instructions with patience. In the back seat, John and Danny huddled together for warmth. Each wore two pairs of pants, two shirts, two pairs of socks, boots and galoshes, with all this topped by heavy Mackinaw coats, scarves, and watch caps. They resembled newsreel images of German soldiers on the Russian Front during the winter of 1941. The boys knew from experience, however, that all this wool wouldn't be proof against the cold once they were in the blinds.

"Russell, you're going too fast! We're going to slide off the road, and then we'll have to hike back to town to get help. Slow down, goddammit!"

This was Uncle Ed's signature oath, and when he invoked it, he did so with panache which gave the phrase weight and substance.

"Don't worry, Ed. These icy ruts are really deep; I couldn't get out of them if I wanted to."

While the two men spun out their good-natured banter, the car bounced along through the predawn darkness. Presently, they came to a long windbreak of junipers planted by the state to keep snow from drifting across the road. The trees were thick and formed a dark, impenetrable wall, barely visible at the edge of the bright cones projected by the Studebaker's headlights.

At this moment, they were approaching the grade crossing of the Santa Fe mainline. Then, in the brief span of four or five seconds, something terrible and amazing happened. As the car climbed up the sloped approach to the tracks, it came out of the shelter of the junipers. Just as the car bestrode the tracks, it was suddenly flooded with blazing light, shaken as by some great roaring, blaring force, until down the other side it chugged. Russell jammed on the brakes, and the car slid to a stop.

"Goddammit! What was *that*?" shouted Uncle Ed, astonished by the blinding light and the noise.

"The Santa Fe Super Chief!" Russell answered, his hands clutching the steering wheel tightly. "We jumped out in front of that train like a jackrabbit out of the weeds."

The uproar completely shocked and confused Danny. But, when he looked out the peep-hole in his frosty window, he saw the red light on the rear of the club car grow dim as the great train hurtled toward distant Los Angeles at eighty miles an hour. With sudden clarity they all understood what just happened. By only a few feet, they had narrowly beaten the Super Chief to the grade crossing in their unwitting race with death. Uncle Ed started laughing, and Russell and the boys joined in.

"You ought to be more careful, Russell," Uncle Ed intoned in a mock-serious voice.

A half hour later, they pulled into the yard of a ramshackle farmhouse. Sonny Albert owned the wheat land where they were going to hunt, and although they already had his permission, hunting manners required calling at his house beforehand. The house was a one-room square, and when the hunters entered, they could see Sonny's wife and several small children huddled in a large bed in one corner. They used a wood burning stove for heat, and the house was pungent with all manner of human smells. Sonny, barefoot and in long johns, insisted they have some coffee, which he preceded to heat on the stove. While the coffee perked, he sloshed water around in some cups to clean them and filled them brimful with the steaming brew.

"The coffee is delicious, Sonny," said Russell. He glanced furtively at the boys, and when he made eye contact with each, his look-message to them said "Drink up!" John swallowed a gulp of the hot, bitter coffee, and then seconded his dad.

"This coffee is really good! Thanks a lot, Mr. Albert."

"So, boys, you're going to shoot yourselves some geese this morning? You won't have to preserve them, because they'll hit the ground froze solid," Sonny teased. Everyone laughed, even Sonny's wife. He wasn't far wrong with the temperature pushing zero.

Despite their primitive dwelling, the Alberts were hospitable and generous. Russell worked hard year round maintaining these relationships that provided access to hunting. It usually involved occasional gifts of bourbon whiskey. The final twirl of this courting dance involved Russell inviting Sonny along on the hunt, to which he demurred, as Russell expected. Nonetheless, the invitation was essential.

"Oh, I'd truly love to go into the fields with you fellows," said Sonny, "but I have to bring up a wagon load of hay for the livestock in the barn. Next time you come down, I'll surely go."

Back in the car, free from the dim squalor of the Albert house, Russell piloted the Studebaker along a tractor road into the sea of winter wheat that receded toward the horizon in every direction. By then, all the stars were gone, and a pale hint of light in the east marked the place where the sun would shortly rise. The car rolled to a stop in a ravine sheltered by a grove of gnarled cottonwoods. Scattered about were an old rusty Farmall tractor squatting on flat tires, a four-bottom plow, and other implements. A car parked among this derelict machinery wouldn't alarm any flights of geese that might pass overhead.

The geese, by the tens of thousands, spent their nights on John Martin Reservoir, a huge impoundment on the Arkansas River which lay about twenty miles to the west. At dawn, the geese would fly for miles over the prairie to wheat fields where they'd alight and feed. Russell scouted out this exact place the previous day, having seen geese feeding here, and chose it for the setup.

The four hunters piled out of the car into the frigid dawn. They stamped their feet and rubbed their hands together with their backs to the wind. Danny realized there would be no respite from the intense cold for the next few hours. Hence, with stoic resignation, he hiked up his scarf and pulled his watch cap down until only a narrow slit remained through which to see. It was important to him to appear not to care, like his dad and Uncle Ed.

"John, in the trunk of the car there's a box of 16 gauge number sixes. Grab a few and load three into your shotgun," said Russell. "We might kick up a cottontail or two, and that would be a fine bonus."

John used the shotgun his parents had given him for his birthday, a 16 gauge Remington Model 11, of which he was inordinately proud. He'd first hunted with it for pheasants in South Dakota the previous November, and he'd become fairly confident in its use. Having gotten the shells, John turned the shotgun over and shoved two shells into the loading port. Then, trying to give the impression of being an old hand, he cycled the bolt with studied casualness and shoved one more shell into the magazine.

"Okay, Dad, I'm ready," he said. This was manly stuff, and in such matters it was important to seem to know the drill.

"Danny," continued Russell, "You bring along the sack of doughnuts and the coffee thermos."

This was boy's work, but having a role in the hunt pleased Danny and made him proud. Only Russell and John would be shooting. Uncle Ed and Danny would be thoughtful observers of the scene and critics of the shooters' performances.

From the car, the blinds were about a mile of hard walking across the snow-dusted rows of wheat. Ten feet separated the two blinds. These consisted of trenches four feet deep in which the hunters could hunker out of the wind. Around the edges of the blinds, the hunters piled up parapets of tumbleweeds to hide their silhouettes. Scattered through the wheat rows around the blinds were several dozen decoys that gave the appearance of a flock of geese feasting on the tender wheat shoots. Ideally, the decoys would attract any birds that flew close enough to this setup to notice.

Russell and Danny climbed into one blind and Uncle Ed and John into the other. The blinds were close enough for the hunters to talk back and forth, the discussion consisting mostly of complaints about the cold and bold predictions about the coming shoot. Gradually, the numbing cold drove the hunters deeper into their foxholes, and a silence fell over the immense prairie, broken only by the sound of the wind.

Danny huddled down out of the wind. A sound like the distant barking of dogs aroused him out of his reverie. He peeked over the edge of the blind and scanned the sky to the west. He saw a thin line just above the horizon that looked like a crack in the dome of the sky. A huge flight of Canada geese, yet several miles away, was winging in their direction.

Russell began speaking softly. Danny listened intently, hoping to understand. Quickly, Danny realized Russell was reciting something to himself. The tone of his dad's voice seemed almost prayerful as he spun out line after line of beautiful words:

> "Whither 'midst falling dew,
> While glow the heavens with the last steps of day,
> Far, through their rosy depths, dost thou pursue
> Thy solitary way?
>
> Vainly the fowler's eye
> Might mark thy distant flight, to do thee wrong,
> As, darkly painted on the crimson sky,
> Thy figure floats along."

Danny realized the words his dad was reciting concerned a wild goose. He began to listen more intently as Russell continued,

> "There is a power, whose care
> Teaches thy way along the pathless coast,
> The desert and illimitable air,
> Lone wandering, but not lost."

Danny was enchanted by his dad's quiet soliloquy. The words had a compelling, powerful beauty.

> "Thou'rt gone, the abyss of heaven
> Hath swallowed up they form; yet, on my heart
> Deeply hath sunk the lesson thou hast given,
> And shall not soon depart.

He, who, from zone to zone,
Guides through the boundless sky thy certain flight,
In the long way that I must trace alone,
Will lead my steps aright."

When his dad finished speaking, Danny asked him about what he'd said.

"Oh, it's a poem I learned as a boy," he answered, "something I've always loved. I like to say it at times like this. It reminds me of things I think are important."

This puzzled Danny. Later in his life, he would come to know and love Bryant's "To a Waterfowl" just like his dad. But, as a twelve-year-old boy crouching in a sandy trench on the Colorado prairie on a bitter cold morning, it was all very mysterious. Years later, he would understand his dad's recitation honored the atavistic bond between the hunter and his quarry.

By this time, the thin line above the horizon dissolved into individual dots, each a goose. The flight aimed right for their setup, and, though not a shooter, Danny sensed keenly the thrill of the chase. Russell had made it clear to John that he shouldn't shoot until his dad began firing. He knew that when the geese set their wings and descended out of the sky into this little ambush, it would be unbearably exciting. The birds would seem as large as B-29s, and a premature shot, precipitated by the avian chaos, would ruin it all.

Danny remained motionless, as his dad had instructed him, while the birds seemed to plummet out of the sky right at him. Suddenly, Russell stood up, swung his shotgun on a big gander, and ... nothing! The great birds were terrified by this apparition out of the weeds and wheeled and fled with a furious cacophony of honking and wing beats. Their departure was foreshadowed in Bryant's poem.

"Thou'rt gone, the abyss of heaven
Hath swallowed up thy form."

Canada Goose
Branta canadensis

Canada Goose Descending into Decoys

It was over in a matter of seconds. The geese came, panicked at the sight of Russell and John, and were now only small distant shapes against the morning sky. Uncle Ed broke the stunned silence.

"Well, goddammit, Russell, did you forget how to shoot that thing?"

"My gun is frozen! I pulled the trigger, and it wouldn't fire!" complained Russell, exasperation in his voice. "The blowing dirt and snow have locked it up."

He then turned to John, still standing with his shotgun at the ready.

"Son, point your gun over the decoys and pull the trigger."

The Model 11 boomed, and the shot column threw up a geyser of snow thirty yards away. Because John had followed his dad's explicit instructions not to shoot early, he'd stood impotently, waiting for the report of Russell's shotgun. One fat goose after another had flown over the sight of his shotgun. The report hadn't come.

Everyone began laughing. The geese had won.

———❖———

That evening, in the Cozy Corner Café in Las Animas, the four companions recounted to each other the events of the day, complete with animated gestures. The family in the adjacent booth gradually entered into the conversation. The man was a farmer, betrayed by his Carhartt coveralls. He laughed repeatedly as the story of the day's hunt unfolded.

"You should come out to my place," he offered. "The damn geese are eating up my winter wheat. Hell, I'll buy your shells for you!"

"Maybe I'll take you up on that," Russell responded. "I could start a business. I'd call it Russell's Goose Eradicators."

"From what I'm hearing," returned the farmer, "You won't have too many customers."

All five of the booths erupted in laughter. Russell, Uncle Ed, John, and Danny realized their conversation had become public property. The farmer got up from his seat and stood in front of the hunters, leaning on the back on the booth.

"My name is George Riesling – like the wine. I'm in the phonebook. You fellows are welcome to come hunt on my place anytime." Then he shook hands with all four and returned to his family's table.

With supper finished, the four hunters climbed back into the Studebaker and headed into the chill, starry night. It was over a hundred miles to Colorado Springs and the welcome warmth of home.

"So, Danny, what do you think about our hunt?" John asked, as the old car hummed down the lonely highway through the winter night.

Danny sat pensively. He thought about the events of the day and composed his answer carefully. He remembered vividly his father's recitation and recalled in particular the words where the poet invoked God's help in the way he would "trace alone." That image awakened in Danny a new idea, that everything – the wheat shoots, the wind, the geese, and Danny himself – has a way to trace. He dimly realized that he, too, danced in the great majestic dance.

"I really learned a lot, not just about hunting geese, but, you know, about life and stuff. The best part was being with you and Dad and Uncle Ed. I guess I don't care that we didn't get any geese. Maybe we will next year. It's hard for me to say what I mean."

True, they'd brought no geese to hand, nor even any cottontails for that matter, but they did have a wonderful day, never to be forgotten. In the coming years, John and Danny would grow into manhood, and Russell and Ed Brinson would decline into old age. But this day, with the blowing snow, the thundering train, Sonny's coffee, the plunging geese, and the mute guns, would remain a treasured memory.

John knew exactly what Danny was struggling to say. He leaned forward and patted his father on the shoulder to get his attention.

"Thanks for taking us with you, Dad. It was a fine hunt."

TEN

DANIEL IN THE LION'S DEN

Dare to be a Daniel,
Dare to stand alone!
Dare to have a purpose firm!
Dare to make it known.
― Phillip Bliss ―

"But, Russ, mountain lions are dangerous!" Louise pleaded.

"I know they are," Russell agreed. "However, the boys won't see any lions. I've hunted all over these mountains for years. In all those hunts, I've only seen two lions, and those were just fleeting glimpses. They're wary and reclusive. I'd say the boys have about as good a chance to hunt up a lion as a snowball has in hell."

"But," she objected, "John is only eighteen and Danny is just a child."

"Come on, now, Louise. John has hunted deer with me for the last two seasons. He knows his way around the woods. He is an excellent shot, and I've drummed the lessons of proper gun-handling into him. As for Danny, I grant he's young, but he and John are close. John will take care of him. They'll be fine."

"I just don't know." Louise was troubled by the dangers a mother would conjure up, dangers that wouldn't occur to a woodsman father.

So began the Great Mountain Lion Hunt. The discussion between Louise and Russell was occasioned by an announcement John made at the supper table earlier in the evening. This whole affair turned on the central fact that a mountain lion had been raiding garbage cans on the west side of town. Colorado Springs lay right up against the Front Range of the Rocky Mountains, and wild animals were frequent visitors to the neighborhoods that edged the foothills. This particular big cat had developed a taste for garbage, and his nighttime visits were frequent enough to make the front page of the *Gazette-Telegraph*.

When John broke the news at supper, he assured his surprised parents he knew exactly where the lion spent its days. There was a long canyon, he explained, which began several miles up in the mountains and wended its way down to the west side of town. At the head of this canyon was an abandoned limestone quarry. He'd visited this place often when target shooting with friends. John figured this maze of artificial caverns would be a perfect lair for the lion. It might hang around the quarry by day, and when night fell, the cat could skulk down the canyon to work its mischief along the edge of town. John was confident he'd figured the matter out down to the least detail, and Danny eagerly seconded every point John made.

For her part, Mary sniffed haughty disdain for the whole enterprise. She had a tender heart and opposed the killing of these beautiful animals. But more to the point, she considered her brother's scheme to be a dangerous fool's errand.

March had arrived, and this one, like most, entered appropriately enough like a lion. KRDO forecast a mix of sunshine and snow for the appointed weekend, just the sort of weather boys would relish for a proper adventure. John planned to leave the tent at home, and in its stead take a large tarp. He intended to rig a lean-to with an extended porch under which the boys might have their fire and stay dry. It all sounded grand to Danny.

John would carry the Model 94 Russell had given him the previous Christmas. He was eager to conduct his first hunt with the handsome Winchester. His dad had fitted a peep sight on John's rifle and converted it from "a phone-book rifle to a beer-can rifle." This suggested an improvement over the fifty-yard accuracy he could normally expect.

With respect to firearms, Danny wasn't a rank novice. When John received his .30-30, Danny inherited his older brother's Remington single-shot .22. Danny became a fine shot through diligent practice. Russell often took the kids to a dry wash east of town where they honed their marksmanship. They shot rifles at targets placed at various distances out to a hundred yards. They also worked on wing shooting, using shotguns on hand-thrown clay pigeons. Danny mastered his .22 so thoroughly that, from a distance of thirty or forty feet, he could hit a fired .22 case placed on the barb of a barbwire fence.

While teaching his kids these skills, Russell also drummed into their minds the manners of proper gun handling. He repeated over and again the stern injunction of his grandfather from many years previous.

"There's only one rule, and you must always follow it," Emanuel had said. "Never point a gun at something you don't intend to shoot. Never."

Russel called this *muzzle consciousness,* and his correction of any infraction fell upon them swiftly and sharply. Thus, in the Gray home, guns weren't squirreled away under lock and key. Russell's rules became second nature to the kids. Firearms couldn't be touched without his supervision or his permission. Padlocks couldn't possibly have the deterrent power of his warnings.

On Friday evening, John cleaned his rifle thoroughly. Where Danny was an apprentice, John was a journeyman. A gulf of skill and learning stood between Danny's little rimfire and John's centerfire carbine. Entranced, Danny sat beside John at the workbench quizzing him on every detail of the mechanism and function of the rifle. John snapped it to his shoulder from time to time, imagining a mountain lion leaping at him from a branch high in a ponderosa. When John satisfied himself with his ministrations, he cycled the action several times, lowered the hammer, and put the rifle in its case.

After protracted delays and several false starts, the boys got under-way around noon on Saturday. The first leg of the journey followed the Rampart Range Road, a gravel road that wound through the foothills in a northerly direction. The second leg involved turning onto a less defined road and following it west over the hills for several miles. Finally, with Frances in four-wheel drive, the boys followed a faint trail that ended at the quarry.

The quarry itself had been excavated from the face of a high limestone bluff with an opening large enough for trucks to enter. Inside the quarry, a maze of tunnels wound through massive rock pillars out of which the quarrymen had taken thousands of tons of limestone rubble over the years. A flat bench spread out from the quarry mouth about fifty yards wide and long. Here the trucks and excavating equipment would have parked during the productive years. From the leading edge of the bench, one could see Colorado Springs six or seven miles below where the canyon gave way to the plains. To John and Danny, this provided the perfect stage for the forthcoming drama.

John selected a flat spot on the bench relatively free of stones and a safe distance from the quarry mouth, ideal for their camp. According to the plan, the cat would be using the quarry for shelter. There were other entrances, and the lion could enter and leave by many routes.

John had learned from his dad the importance of careful observation when in the backcountry. Russell frequently counseled the boys to make a thorough inspection of the area surrounding a campsite as soon as the camp was up. By this he meant they should scout the adjacent landscape to locate water, animal trails, dangers, and the like. One did this by careful walking and attentive looking. In this spirit, John and Danny set out from their camp, like the bear that went over the mountain, to see what they could see.

Their scout turned up two very interesting discoveries. A quarter-mile from camp, half hidden in a thicket of scrub oak, the boys found a long abandoned Model A Ford pickup. The old truck was completely intact and squatted in wistful decrepitude. The tires were reduced to rotted rings of rubber, and the paint was completely gone leaving an overall patina of rust. The glass shone intact in the cab windows. Still present, as well, were the steering wheel, gauges, and bench seat. John and Danny immediately hatched a plan for another expedition to drag this old girl back home and restore her to her former glory. They had no real idea of the difficulties such a scheme entailed, but they were young and imaginative in a world full of possibility.

The second discovery was more sobering. They decided to enter the quarry in order to see what lay beyond the gaping tunnel mouth. Several inches of powdered limestone, with the consistency and fineness of gray flour, covered the floor of the quarry. This natural canvas told an ominous tale. Everywhere they looked they saw the unmistakable tracks of a mountain lion. John's hunch proved correct. This quarry made a perfect lair for a lion bent on raiding the garbage cans of Colorado Springs. The cat might well be watching them at this very moment. This frightened Danny, and he stepped closer to John who was now carrying his .30-30 at port arms. All around the boys, a labyrinth of cavernous chambers and passages gloomed in the half-light.

"Cock the hammer," John said softly to himself, "shoulder the rifle, see the cat over the barrel and shoot."

John swept the quarry with his eyes. There were dark passages, rock pillars, and heaps of rubble, any of which might conceal a crouching lion poised to spring.

"Okay, Danny," John whispered. "Turn around slowly and head for the daylight. Whatever you do, don't run! If he's watching us, running might make him attack."

Danny, thoroughly terrified, tried to walk nonchalantly. He also tried to whistle, but his dry lips could only make a musical buzz. When they emerged into the afternoon light, the boys grinned at each other sheepishly, surprised by the intensity of their fear. Since the beginning of this great adventure, the mountain lion was a kind of abstraction living on the boundary of imagination. Seeing its tracks in the gray dust, however, made the lion suddenly and fiercely real.

———◆———

Back at their camp, John laid out for Danny his plan for bagging the big cat. John figured it probably left the quarry at night, worked its way down the canyon, and crept around in the outskirts of the sleeping town searching for food. Then, John reasoned, once sated, the lion would return to the quarry when dawn broke. The fact of the cat's increasing boldness meant it was losing its fear of humans. Consequently, it wouldn't regard human sign around their camp as inherently dangerous. He explained that their best chance would be to lie in wait atop a large rubble pile near the quarry mouth. This spot would provide a great view of the approaches to the quarry and an excellent shooting point should the lion arrive.

Having put the tactical question to rest, John declared suppertime, and the boys settled into the age-old rhythm of life in a hunting camp. Their mother had prepared a pot of chili for them to take along. They heated it over the fire and wolfed it down with the aid of cheese bread, all washed down by hot chocolate.

After supper, camp routine required a detailed analysis of the events of the day. That afternoon, the boys had two remarkable experiences that were very different. Danny felt overwhelmed by this abundance of *coolness*. That meant their discussion would revolve around two principal topics: saving the old Ford truck and hunting the lion. These two topics provoked Danny into nonstop, eager conversation with his older brother.

"How will we get the truck to roll?" asked Danny.

"I'll get some wheels and tires from a junk yard," answered John.

"How will we pull it?"

"With a chain."

"Who will steer the truck?"

"I will."

"Who will drive Frances?"

"Dad."

Then, there ensued a lengthy mechanical dissertation by John on the intricacies of restoring the truck based on his recent work on Frances. Ignoring John's sketchy pedigree as a mechanic, Danny imagined himself cruising around Colorado Springs in this old pickup reborn through John's craft. Having settled that, the conversation shifted to hunting.

"Could you shoot an elephant with your .30-30?" asked Danny.

"I could shoot one, but it would be a really dumb idea. Elephant hunters use huge rifles, much more powerful than mine."

"Well, could it kill a polar bear?"

"Lots of big bears have been killed with the .30-30 over the years, but it wouldn't be my first choice."

"We could drive Frances to Alaska and hunt bears!" enthused Danny, undeterred.

"Alaska is far away, and Frances is pretty small to carry all the stuff we'd need."

"But we could!" Danny persisted, mingling as he often did possibility and probability.

"There's one important thing you must understand, Danny," John cautioned. "Dad always says the only reason to kill animals is for food. Shooting them just to put their heads on your den wall is called trophy hunting, and Dad thinks it's dead wrong."

"Well, we're not going to eat this lion," Danny countered.

"You're right. But Dad says it's okay to kill animals that are a danger to you or other people. I guess that covers us hunting this lion."

"But the lion wasn't a danger to us until we came up here, was he?" Danny pressed.

John sat silently. His younger brother had made a nice point, and in truth, John had felt vaguely uneasy about their lion hunt from its inception for this very reason.

"You know, he *is* a problem lion," John continued, heavily accenting the *is*. "He has grown used to humans from having spent a lot of time hanging around the edge of town. That makes him doubly dangerous; he has probably lost his fear of people. I think it's all right for us to kill him, although now that we're up here in his country, I don't feel as strongly about shooting him as I did back home reading the newspaper."

John recognized in himself what Aldo Leopold once described as being young and full of "trigger itch." His certainty about the correctness of his original view waned under the simple force of his brother's logic. In addition, the magnitude of his dilemma increased by being alone in rugged country on a stormy night with responsibility for a twelve-year-old boy. This project didn't seem nearly so romantic as it had around the supper table.

"Let's play it by ear, Danny," John concluded. "After a good night's sleep, we'll see how it goes.

This cliché didn't resolve John's moral paradox, but his temporizing left room for God or Fate or Nature to reveal the paths that he, Danny, and the mountain lion should take.

Shortly thereafter, the wind rose, sifting fine snow upon the two brothers warming themselves by their night fire high up this wild canyon. The onset of the snow reminded them they needed shelter. They abandoned John's lean-to plan for lack of adequate poles to prop up the tarp, and improvised. They laid the ten feet by sixteen feet tarp on the ground, rolled out their bedrolls on it, and doubled the tarp back over their heads, sealing themselves in a canvas envelope. Where the top of the tarp and the bottom came together there were many small gaps that provided ventilation. The tarp was waxy and stiff, and Danny made a little dome above his head for breathing space. It surprised him how warm and comfortable they were in their jury-rigged sleeping arrangement. Danny was particularly comforted by John lying right next to him. He regarded John to be a master of all the manly skills he hoped to possess someday. He also knew John's rifle lay between the two of them. Dawn would bring a bright new day.

"See you in the morning," Danny whispered.

"Yeah, we'll be fine. It's only going to snow three or four inches. Goodnight, Danny. See you in the morning."

Lying beside his brother in the darkness under the tarp, Danny thought about their planned ambush of the lion. It made him uneasy. After all, the lion followed his own path, about which the big cat had no choice. Tomorrow morning, if all went according to plan, the boys' paths and the lion's would merge inexorably into one.

In this solitary meditation, a feeling akin to sorrow moved Danny. To allay his worry, Danny recited his night prayers so as to reassure

Mountain Lion
Puma concolor

Mountain Lion in Snowy Landscape

himself that all was well. As an altar boy at St. Mary's, he'd learned a few prayers in Latin. Thus, tonight, he recited an *Ave Maria* and a *Pater Noster* with unusual earnestness. Danny didn't know the latter prayer completely through, but he did his best, finishing it in English. He trusted God wouldn't hold this polyglot effort against him. Just before falling asleep he said, "Night, Johnny."

The silently falling snow gradually clothed the trees and hills with a white mantle. After several hours, the storm passed, and the moon beamed upon a silvery world. Frances appeared to be a snow covered boulder. The boys under the tarp were indistinguishable from the ground upon which they lay. Their camp became part of the landscape.

Far into the night, when the mountain lion climbed up onto the bench in front of the quarry swinging its head back and forth in the crystal air, no human scent betrayed the sleeping boys. Like a shadowy wraith, the regal cat padded softly over the snowy bench, across the snow-covered tarp, past the fire ring, and past Frances toward the quarry entrance. The great cat paused there, turning back briefly to gaze at its moonlit kingdom and then disappeared into the black emptiness.

A profound silence lay upon everything. The lights of Colorado Springs twinkled far below like a fairy world. The wheeling stars shone above as Orion and Taurus, locked in their timeless struggle, drifted slowly west.

—————❖—————

Dawn broke with the spare beauty of a winter morning. Horizon to horizon, a cloudless sky arched overhead. John was awakened by the intense light that filtered through the tarp and snow atop himself and Danny. He threw back the tarp, taking care to keep snow out of their bed. Everywhere he looked the circumfulgent light was dazzling. He felt like the man newly emerged from Plato's cave. Then, with his hand shading his eyes, he saw the story written across their snow-covered bed, and it startled him.

"Danny, wake up!" he called out hoarsely, astonished by the lion tracks. "The lion walked right over us last night!"

Frances drifted slowly south downgrade on the Rampart Range Road. The morning sun quickly melted the night's snowfall. Both John and Danny were pensive, each lost in his own thoughts about the strange and wonderful happenings at their hunting camp.

"We were lucky!" Danny blurted out, breaking the silence.

"Yes, we were," agreed John. "I still can't believe we didn't wake up when the lion walked over us. Had we awakened, it might have been Katie, bar the door!"

"What does that mean?"

"It means things could have gotten really ugly."

"But you had your rifle!"

"It would have been useless if we'd sat up in the darkness with a startled mountain lion standing on top of us."

They both fell back into thoughtful silence as Frances rolled along. The view occasionally opened up so they could see out of the mountains. The Colorado prairie swept eastward endlessly, all the way to the horizon.

"Look at the plains, Danny. You can see forever."

"Yeah, it's like the end of the world is out there, and we can almost see it," Danny countered. "That's kind of like life. I can see way back into my life, but I can't see much ahead. Like with the lion; we thought we knew exactly how to get him. But it turned out so differently."

"Damn, Danny. You're becoming a philosopher!" said John, kidding his brother. "I'm going to start calling you Socrates."

Danny watched the passing landscape and realized his heart was happy. The mountain lion still haunted the canyon, as it surely would for years. Hunters would probably never kill it, only time would. For his part, Danny had kept to his path, and the lion, its own. John, lost in his own thoughts, steered Frances as she rattled and chugged down the muddy road toward home.

ELEVEN

GRANDMA RUTH'S STORIES

O you daughters of the west!
O you young and elder daughters!
O you mothers and you wives!
Never must you be divided, in our ranks you move united.
Pioneers! O pioneers!
– Walt Whitman –

By the end of April, spring, verdant and soft, lay upon the mountains and plains. On the slopes of Cheyenne Mountain, isolated groves of aspen flourished, clad in that exquisite golden green Robert Frost called nature's "hardest hue to hold." The rushing torrents coming down from the Rampart Range – Turkey Creek, Beaver Creek, Cheyenne Creek, Fountain Creek – carried the precious benediction of last winter's snow. More than any other season, springtime in the Rockies presaged a rare and perfect confluence of earth, air, sun, and water. In the cottonwood groves along the creeks and in the forested canyons higher up, birdsong lilted both day and night.

On a Friday evening, the phone rang in the Gray kitchen.

"It's Grandma," said Mary, handing the phone to her mom.

For the next several minutes, mother-in-law and daughter-in-law chatted amiably. The giveaway to the rest of the family, who were all eavesdropping, was Louise's concluding comment.

"A picnic would be wonderful! Let's plan on leaving about ten."

Picnics were a Colorado Springs institution. The city maintained picnic grounds in several of the wooded canyons that spilled down from the range. In addition, Austin Bluffs, a jumble of forested sandstone bluffs on the prairie east of town, provided a fine choice with similar amenities. The Gray's favorite picnic place lay several miles up North Cheyenne Canyon along the Gold Camp Road. Right where the road made a hairpin turn and crossed the creek, a pull-off under tall ponderosas offered a sturdy table and a fire ring. It was far enough into the mountains that they could always count on finding it unoccupied. This would be the site of Saturday's spring picnic.

———◦—◦◦—◦———

As if by design, Saturday's forecast promised fine weather all day. With the food and other necessities loaded into the back of the station wagon, Russell driving, Louise and Grandma Ruth in the front seat and the kids in back, the Gray family set out for the Gold Camp Road.

The first chore after unloading the car involved scouring the surrounding forest for firewood. The adults lounged in camp chairs drinking coffee while the kids built up a pile of wood. People rarely used this place, so fallen limbs and deadfall lay strewn about. Before long, John, Mary, and Danny had amassed more than enough fuel for the cook fire. Then Russell began working his magic.

First came the time-consuming task of frying the potatoes. Russell mounded up the large potato slices in his well-seasoned, cast-iron skillet, patiently turning and stirring them until golden brown. Setting these aside, he fried bacon and sausage, and, finally, scrambled eggs fortified with hot pepper sauce.

Louise spread her checkered red table cloth to cover the weathered wood of the table. With the places set, she laid out the platters of potatoes, meat, and eggs. The family said grace, and Grandma Ruth, still a faithful Methodist, pronounced an additional blessing. For the next half-hour, everyone enjoyed the ample breakfast, passing the platters back and forth, filling and refilling cups of coffee, and nattering happily. John then turned the conversation to family history, a subject in which he'd recently become interested.

"Grandma, how did Great Grandpa Fleisher end up living on the Kansas prairie? I thought he was a preacher. There wouldn't be many people there to preach to. Wasn't that Indian country?"

"Well, Johnny, let me draw a picture for you. In 1872, Papa filed a homestead claim at the Land Office in Topeka. This claim entitled him to three-hundred and twenty acres of unbroken prairie in Smith County, just south of the Nebraska line. If he lived on it for five years and did the assessment work, it would eventually be deeded to him. Spring Creek meandered across his land that, despite its name, carried no water except after heavy rains. Papa hoped there would be some timber scattered along the creek, but the only tree on his claim was a forlorn old box elder that grew on a small knoll a short distance from the creek. A log cabin was out of the question.

"The vertical creek banks stood fifteen feet high which allowed him to excavate a dugout for their dwelling. Papa shoveled until he'd dug a cave about twelve feet deep, twelve feet wide, and seven feet high. He bought a wagon load of planks in Smith Center, the nearest town, to close off the front. Your great grandmother, Lucy, had carried a foot square pane of glass on her lap all the way from Topeka. She told Papa they must have a window in their prairie home. The glass became a small window in the front door.

"The sandy ground typical of the Solomon River Valley formed the walls. Papa whitewashed them, which gave them the appearance of plaster. They furnished the room sparsely. I remember it well. A large bed filled the back corner with a small table beside it. On the table were a coal oil lamp and Papa's Bible. The cook stove stood against the far wall. Papa bored a hole down through the earth atop the dugout until it pierced the ceiling. The stovepipe connected the stove to the hole. If you walked across the prairie, you would've seen smoke curling up out of the ground. Of course, Papa affixed some cabinets and racks to the walls where things might be stored."

"But what about the Indians," John pressed.

"When Papa and Mama settled into their dugout home, the Cheyenne still roamed over most of Kansas and Nebraska. Of course, we didn't think of the land as populated, since the Indians were nomads and moved about constantly following the buffalo herds. I realize now, seventy-five years later, that the land truly belonged to them as it had for hundreds of years. But people didn't see it that way back then.

"Papa's family immigrated from Germany, and all the Germans coming into the United States believed the prairie was unpopulated and free for the taking. For the first several years, Papa and Mama saw Indians regularly, and on one occasion a party of Cheyenne warriors came riding up Spring Creek. When Papa went out to meet them, they responded menacingly; however, they didn't try to force an entry into our home. They did shoot our cow, however. Soon after that incident, the government forced their tribe onto a reservation in Oklahoma, and we never saw the Cheyenne again.

"You are right. It does seem odd for a Methodist preacher to be farming on the Kansas prairie, but Papa needed a livelihood, and he descended from farmers. After a few years, when more people settled on the prairie, Papa rode a regular circuit of about two-hundred miles, preaching and serving small congregations in the towns springing up.

"The first several years were very difficult. Papa and Mama had six children on the homestead, but only three survived infancy: my older brothers, Sumner and Ernest, and I. Life was hard, and many unexpected and discouraging things happened. Despite these tragedies, Papa always had hope.

"Once, a man who called himself an atheist asked Papa why he believed in God. Papa answered him, 'Believe in God? Why, I've known Him personally for forty years.'"

Grandma Ruth sat quietly, as if gazing into the past. In a little while, she spoke again.

"One bitterly cold winter night, Papa awoke to a smoke-filled room. He lit the coal oil lamp and got up to check the stove. When he opened the stoking door, he yelled and jumped back as a tangled mass of rattlesnakes tumbled onto the floor. It was frightening to see them writhing and spreading out in the dim light of the lamp. Mama cried, and we children were terrified. When Papa recovered from his initial shock, he threw open the dugout door, fetched a rake that leaned against the front wall of the dugout, and dragged the snakes out onto the creek bed where they froze to death. The next day, Papa skinned them, and Mama used the meat in a delicious soup she made with potatoes, dried corn, and beans.

"Later, Papa figured out what had happened. Apparently, his chimney hole passed close to a jack rabbit burrow. The rattlesnakes hibernated in this burrow and they somehow burst through into the chimney hole, drawn by the heat. They fell down into the stove, choking the stove fire and causing the room to fill with smoke. Several burned to death on the coals, but the others burst out the stove door when Papa opened it.

"Papa tanned several snake skins and mama used the leather to make a pair of suspenders for him. It was difficult because the skins were thicker and tougher than cloth; pushing a needle through them required strength and care. Papa was uncommonly proud of these, and, although not a vain man, he loved to wear them as he preached. When he really got into a sermon, he would take off his coat dramatically, and these snakeskin suspenders would usually draw a surprised gasp from the worshippers. Of course, he could only work that ploy once on a congregation, but since he served an extensive circuit of Methodist churches scattered over several counties, he had ample opportunities."

"Did you see the snakes, Grandma?" asked Danny excitedly.

"No," she replied. "I was just a baby. But Papa told me the story many times, and I imagine it so vividly, it now seems as if I saw it all."

"Grandma, when you lived on the Kansas homestead, where did you get food?" asked Danny.

"Well, Danny, we didn't have much variety of food at the time. Papa farmed about ten acres of sweet corn, and Mama put out a large garden. We dried most of the corn after harvest, and then it could be cooked in soup or ground into meal. Mama made wonderful cornbread, baking a batch every few weeks. We also ate fried cornmeal mush as a breakfast staple. Her garden provided a cornucopia of fresh vegetables in season.

"A little grove of chokecherry trees flourished on the creek bottom about a mile away. I can still taste the wonderful flavor of the jelly Mama made. It always seemed miraculous that such a bitter, puckery fruit could make such a delicious treat. Papa also dug a root cellar where turnips, carrots, and potatoes could be kept through the winter months.

"Game abounded on the prairie and in the wooded draws. Papa hunted frequently in the fall and winter. Cottontails, jack rabbits, prairie chickens, and quail provided meat, along with a deer from time to time. But let me tell you about a strange thing that happened, both frightening and thrilling, which fed our family for an entire winter.

"One fall day, Papa was harvesting corn, which he did by pulling off the ears, then cutting the stalks and stacking them in shocks. He bent over continually while cutting the corn, and he attended carefully to his work so that he wouldn't injure himself with the big corn knife. Whenever he worked in the field, he slung his shotgun over his shoulder in case he scared up a rabbit or a covey of quail. What he spooked up, however, wasn't a rabbit.

"Working the corn knife and stacking the stalks, perhaps composing a sermon in his mind, he looked up to find himself facing a bull buffalo no more than ten yards away. With the buffalo also quietly doing its own harvesting, the two of them met by surprise. The buffalo snorted, his tail stood up, and he pawed the ground. Papa thought it would probably charge him, so he pulled his shotgun off his shoulder and emptied both barrels into the buffalo's chest. This didn't kill the animal, but only enraged it. Papa knew he had only one chance, namely, to climb up our lone tree. Papa got to the tree just ahead of the buffalo, jumped, grabbed a limb, and swung up out of reach. He'd thrown his useless gun down during his flight. Mama, Sumner, Ernest, and I watched in fear from the door of the dugout as the drama unfolded.

"The buffalo butted the tree repeatedly, then milled about, and finally lay down. Although Papa's two shots eventually caused the buffalo to bleed to death, it took several hours before he could come down out of the tree. This provided a food bonanza for us. Papa butchered the buffalo, and dried the meat Indian-style. That big bull fed our family for most of the winter.

"Years later, after we moved to town, Sumner visited the site of the homestead. The box elder tree was gone, but the stump remained. He took a chunk of wood to the town of Burr Oak, and a cabinet maker there milled a small tablet out of it. Papa wrote the story of the buffalo and his harrowing escape on the wooden tablet. I still have it."

"How long did you live on the homestead, Grandma," asked Danny, "and where did you go to school?"

"When I was eight, we sold the homestead. Mama died the previous year after giving birth to their last child. Living there any longer became too difficult. We left because Papa got a call to minister to a congregation in Osborne, a town about twenty miles from the homestead. I remember pulling away. I sat in the wagon next to Papa. After about a half-mile, at the crest of a rise, he reined in the horses. Looking back, we could see the box elder tree and the headstones of our family graves. Tears streamed down Papa's face.

"Papa and Mama had seen to our schooling on the homestead, but now I attended classes in a one-room schoolhouse. Going to school with other children frightened me at first, but I soon made friends and came to love Osborne, my girlhood home.

"Eventually, Papa bought a farm on the North Fork of the Gunnison River in Colorado at the base of Orchard Mesa. He called it Beulah Land – a land of milk and honey – after the place God promised the Israelites when they left Babylon. For Papa, everything had to be rooted in the Bible. Anyway, we lived there for many years. I met and married Lincoln, and we had a baby we named Russell. Lincoln died when Russell was six."

Grandma Ruth turned and smiled at Russell, her only child. Her love for him was obvious.

As for Russell, his relationship with his mom had been stormy over the years. When a young man, Russell chafed under the strictures of his mother and grandfather, and he felt burdened by their expectations.

Homestead Cemetery, Smith County, Kansas

His errant years during the Great Depression worried her, and only in recent years had the two reached an accommodation.

"What happened to Sumner and Ernest, Grandma?" Mary asked, pulling the conversation back to the homestead stories. "Why didn't they move with you to Colorado?"

"It's a very sad story, Mary," Grandma Ruth answered. "I will never get through it dry-eyed. But their story is also mysterious and wonderful, as you will hear. It begins when we were still living in Osborne. Papa's brother, Sim, owned a farm in Michigan. An aged aunt who was *non compos mentis* lived with his family."

John picked up on the Latin. "That means she'd lost her mind," he said proudly.

"Yes, that's true," Grandma Ruth responded. "They needed to do everything for her – feed her, bathe her, dress her – everything. This was always difficult, but even more so in summer when everyone worked in the fields. Hence, Uncle Sim wrote Papa and asked if I might take the train back to Michigan and be her companion for the summer. This would allow the other folks to get the crops in. I was excited to go. When Sumner and Ernest returned from college in the spring, they immediately went to work with a harvesting crew. This would keep them away from home for the entire summer until their classes resumed in the fall. Home was so lonely.

"My summer in Michigan began very peacefully. I spent every day on the front porch of the farmhouse with Aunt Anna. She sat in a wheelchair, and I cared for all her needs. Really, it wasn't unpleasant. I enjoyed a lovely view from the porch. The Michigan landscape seemed much more lush and green than our Kansas prairie. I spent most of the day reading to her. I went through several novels and much Scripture. She always looked straight ahead and made neither a sound nor a gesture.

"One day in late August, something very strange happened, which I shall never forget. While I was reading to Aunt Anna, she suddenly turned to face me and said, 'Ruthie! I can see Sumner and Ernest. They are far out on the Fields of Glory!' It shocked me.

I had no idea what her words meant. Two days later, it all became clear. A Western-Union messenger delivered a telegram to Uncle Sim. The sheet of yellow paper carried a terrible message from Papa: Sumner and Ernest had both died of pneumonia within a week of each other. I cried for days. My brothers were more than heroes to me; they were gods." She touched the corners of her eyes with a paper napkin. "I couldn't believe they were gone."

Russell immediately rose from his chair and knelt on the ground in front of his mother. He took her hands in his. "It's all right to cry, Mother. God's plan is inscrutable. Look at it this way: only one Fleisher child made it out of Kansas, yet, look around you. I, my kids – we all come from Grandpa Emanuel and from you. We're the milk and honey that the Bible promised."

By mid-afternoon, the shadowed canyon echoed the mood of Grandma Ruth's last story. Louise seized the moment.

"I brought along a deck of cards. Let's play Scotch Bridge! The losers will have to pack everything up."

Her challenge broke the spell. Everyone promptly took places around the picnic table, joking and bragging about who would be the star. Louise broke out a plate of chocolate chip cookies for the kids to dip in their coffee. All was well.

The Gray kids had heard these stories in a general and unfocused way at various family gatherings, but as small children they hadn't paid much attention. However, Grandma's moving rendition at the picnic in Cheyenne Canyon left a deep impression on them.

That night, lying in bed, Danny imagined what it would be like to live in a dirt cave on the prairie and see the Cheyenne scouts riding up Spring Creek. Did those things really happen, he wondered? It was long ago. Yet Grandma Ruth, at a picnic table in 1957, described how she'd seen Indians kill their family's cow. He realized time is like a moving shadow, so elusive and evanescent. He thought about her brothers, Sumner and Ernest. What would their lives have been like if they'd survived pneumonia? He couldn't see them as old like Grandma. In his imagination they were frozen in their hale, strong years.

"Johnny, are you still awake?" Danny whispered.

"What is it?"

"Grandma's life has been really hard, hasn't it?"

"Yeah, it has. I guess I didn't realize just how hard it's been for her until she told us her stories today."

"Well, why do some people have so much sorrow and others so little? Look at our family; our life couldn't be better, and I couldn't be happier."

"That's true, but remember, things change. I'll bet when Grandma was a girl sitting on the porch of the farmhouse in Michigan, she never dreamed the telegram would come with its terrible message. Father Stevins called it the 'Problem of Providence.' Believe me, it's complicated. In the end, I guess, you just have to trust. The way things turn out will either make sense or not. For me, I would rather believe they will. But, man, I sure don't know."

After some silence, Danny said, "I guess that's what Sister Doloretta meant by a mystery. She said there are some things you just can't understand."

"So true," John said quietly, "so true."

TWELVE

THE GHOST TRAIN OF MARSHALL PASS

Life is like a mountain railroad, with an engineer that's brave;
We must make the run successful, from the cradle to the grave.
– M. E. Abbey –

Danny remembered Grandpa Patrick McNally only vaguely. During Danny's childhood, Grandpa visited the Gray home several times. In the box of family photographs, there's a snapshot of Grandpa Patrick sitting on the front porch of the Gray's Monument Street house. In the photograph, he holds Danny on his lap, and Danny is looking up into his grandpa's face adoringly. From those brief visits, Danny retained only one strong memory: Grandpa smoked a curved briar pipe, and he smelled of tobacco smoke. In his memory, this smell of pipe smoke was aromatic and pleasing.

Grandpa smoked Prince Albert tobacco which came in a tin can shaped like a large deck of cards. These cans had hinged tops, and kids loved them as repositories for treasured things much like Plains Indians carrying medicine bags filled with totemic objects. On his last visit, Grandpa had given Danny a Prince Albert can when he'd used up all the tobacco. The can connected him to his grandpa, and eventually it became his fishing box. He loved how it held everything he needed, being just big enough to hold a spare leader, several flies, a small scissors, a tin of floatant, and still fit neatly into his pocket.

Danny saw Grandpa McNally for the last time during the winter of his sixth year. The Grays had driven to Denver to visit Grandpa in the old folks' home where he resided. Danny would always remember the sunlit parlor and the beautiful tableau of his mom bending over the seated figure of her father. When she'd whispered the words, "Papa, it's me, Louise," Grandpa had slowly lifted his head, smiled, and nodded in affirmation. Several weeks thereafter he died.

Louise limned the personality of Grandpa Patrick McNally through stories she illustrated with photographs she'd saved and cherished. The content of most of these stories featured Grandpa's life as a locomotive engineer. She took pride in this. She was an immigrant's child, and in her mind her father's occupation was solid, even noble, and thoroughly American. In many of her stories, she described Grandpa as a heroic figure. When family conversation turned to such stories, Danny imagined a massive steam locomotive hurtling along the rails. He could almost see Grandpa at the throttle, leaning out of the cab window, scanning the track ahead.

The reality, of course, was more prosaic. Patrick McNally had been an upstanding member of the Brotherhood of Locomotive Engineers for most of his adult life. Although he possessed an impeccable work record, it consisted mostly of hauling freight across the mountains for thirty years practically without incident. His private life was sad and difficult, having lost his beloved Brigid early in their marriage. Subsequently, he raised their seven children by himself.

One story, though, always made Louise and her sisters roll their eyes. Grandpa, like many Irish workmen of his era, enjoyed a drop of the dew from time to time. According to this story, whenever his train lay over for a couple of hours in Colorado Springs, a dry town, Patrick and his crew would walk the several miles west to Colorado City where the saloons were many and accommodating. The rest of the story featured a freight train and its transit through precipitous mountain country with the engineer and fireman lustily singing old Irish songs to the syncopated beat of the steam cylinders and thunderous thumping of the exhaust. Thus, it came as no surprise to Russell and Louise that the kids had an interest in the historic railroads of Colorado, particularly the narrow gauge lines.

During the mining booms of the late nineteenth century, most of the trackage in Colorado was laid in narrow gauge. Narrow gauge tracks, with three feet between the rails, could ascend steeper grades and negotiate sharper curves than American standard gauge, with its spacing of four feet, eight and one-half inches.

A romantic aura surrounded narrow gauge railroading, its diminutive locomotives and rolling stock, and the spectacular terrain these trains traversed. As time went on, the railroads converted most of their narrow gauge trackage to standard gauge. The last vestiges of the narrow gauge lines were found only in the most forbidding mountain country. For these reasons, the narrow gauge rights-of-way were especially interesting to the Gray kids.

Often, when John, Mary, and Danny were on one of their mountain expeditions, they'd pull Frances off the road and hike across the expanse of a mountain valley to an abandoned railroad grade. At such times, they collected relics of the railroad days – rusty tie-plates, spikes, and bolts – many of which were strewn along these abandoned rights-of-way.

One of their favorite sites was in South Park. In the heyday of Colorado railroading, several different lines threaded their way across South Park on their way to Leadville and the passes across the Continental Divide. Just beyond Hartzel, for example, the mainline of the Denver, South Park, and Pacific tracks crossed under those of the Colorado Midland. All that remained of this crossing, however, were the roadbeds, stripped of their rails.

Such places were prime hunting ground for artifacts. The kids dreamed of finding a bonanza like their cousin, David, who came upon a wrecked locomotive in a timbered canyon below Boreas Pass. He returned later to the wreck with some tools, detached the brass bell, and brought it out of the canyon. They were sure such a spectacular find awaited them just around the next bend. Their finds, though more modest, were prized nonetheless. Once home, they added these artifacts to their railroad museum in the basement.

———◆———

Of all the stories from Colorado's railroad past, the three kids loved best the tale about the ghost train of Marshall Pass. It was a great story, replete with darkness, danger, and death, featuring a runaway train that jumped the track on the west side of Marshall Pass.

In the days when rail transport was critical to the state's mining economy, Marshall Pass became a major crossing of the Continental Divide. It was notorious among trainmen because of its steep grades and sharp curves. Engineers broke cold sweats when they eased their trains over the summit of the pass and started down the long descent. Such trains would be made up of heavy cars, each weighing many tons, steel wheels rolling on steel rails. Managing such a juggernaut demanded skill. Air brakes weren't yet installed on all railroads, and certainly not on small lines far from major population centers. Hence, the engineer couldn't directly control the brakes, but had to rely on the skill and courage of his brakemen.

Every train carried several brakemen who were responsible for setting the brakes on the cars when the engineer signaled with his whistle. The process of setting the brakes was complicated and difficult. Upon a whistled signal, the brakemen would leave the caboose, climb on top of the cars, and, moving from car to car, set the brakes on each. They did this by turning a wheel that projected above the car roof. This time-consuming process had to be accomplished while the train rolled along, faster and faster, rocking back and forth. It was doubly dangerous at night because the brakemen might be struck by tree limbs or peeled off the train as it plunged into a tunnel. If they were too slow, if the train were too heavy, if the rails were slick with snow and ice, a train could become a runaway.

According to the story, when an engineer named Edwards pulled a passenger train over Marshall Pass, a phantom train chased him down the grade and overtook his train. He claimed to have seen the face of the spectral engineer as the ghost train vaulted over his own and then plunged into the dark canyon, never to be found. According to the legend, engineer Edwards discovered a message scratched in the frost on the cab window of his locomotive the next morning. It warned him that if he pulled a train over Marshall Pass again, his train would run away, and he would be killed.

From time to time through the years, hunters and fishermen reported seeing a phantom train on the Marshall Pass grade. The reports were tantalizing, and they all told the same story, that is, these men had witnessed a train, always at night, roaring down the grade, headlamp glaring, and sparks churning from the locomotive's stack. One such report would've been derided as foolishness. However, to people who noticed such things, these Ghost Train accounts popped up with a vexing regularity and came from local men of experience and probity.

John came across the story in a book on ghost towns he borrowed from the Colorado Springs Public Library. He was instantly captivated. That evening, he told the story of the phantom train at the supper table.

"Mom, did Grandpa pull trains over Marshall Pass?" he asked.

"Yes, he did," she replied. "He used to haul empty hoppers to Utah and return with a coal train to the steel mill in Pueblo. Papa loved the Third Division of the D&RG. He called the descent from the summit of Marshall Pass into the Gunnison Valley the most thrilling thing a locomotive engineer might ever experience."

John glanced at Mary, and then at Danny. It wouldn't be long until they were on their way to Marshall Pass.

———

That expedition, with the kids and their gear packed into Frances, began on a sunny Saturday morning in late June of 1957. The railroad had been scrapped the previous year, and the State converted the roadbed into a gravel auto road. Not only would there be ghost trains in the offing, but Marshall Creek and the beaver ponds on the west side of the pass promised excellent fishing. Hopes were high and hearts happy as Frances chugged down the highway toward the Arkansas River Valley.

The Marshall Creek Valley

Like almost all passes over the Continental Divide, the eastern ascent of Marshall Pass is longer than the more abrupt western descent. The climb begins where the old roadbed crosses Highway 285, a few miles south of Poncha Springs. At first, the landscape is dominated by sedimentary rock, principally sandstone, clothed with a piñon-juniper forest. Igneous rocks begin to dominate as the road climbs through stands of aspen, lodge pole pine, and Engelmann spruce. Finally, near the summit, amid a panorama of rocky peaks, there remain only thin stands of subalpine fir. The landscape on the west side of the pass is a mirror image, and, strikingly, the road winds through two extremely tight curves several miles below the summit. It doesn't take much effort to imagine the terror in the locomotive cab of a runaway train hurtling into the Millhouse Creek curve.

In late afternoon, the kids crossed the 11,800 ft. summit of the pass, dropped down the west side into the timbered valley, and pitched their camp in an aspen grove beside the old railroad grade. While Mary made preparations for supper, John and Danny were able to get in an hour of fishing before sundown.

The creek swarmed with German browns, an exotic European trout imported into America in the nineteenth century. Nearly all the creeks of the Gunnison River drainage had populations of brown trout. They were wary fish, a great challenge for a fly fisherman.

On this lovely summer evening, the browns of Marshall Creek provided John and Danny with an unforgettable memory. Although the fishing started slowly, about half an hour before sunset, a hatch of mayflies sent the trout into a feeding frenzy, and until the disk of the sun dropped below the distant peaks of the San Juan Mountains, the boys hooked a fine, fat trout with nearly every cast.

Later, with supper finished and the dishes washed, the kids stashed their food box in Frances as a precaution against bears and porcupines. Their camp prepared for night, the three sat around their crackling aspen wood fire and engaged in a disputation about the likelihood of seeing the phantom train. John had his doubts. Mary, though doubtful, stayed open to the possibility. Danny was a true believer.

In his mind, it wasn't a question of whether, but of when. A simple dichotomy presented itself: would the three see the spectral train while gathered around their campfire, or would the apparition burst out of the dark night while they slept in their tent?

"Danny," John intoned authoritatively, "remember only a few people have actually seen the train. It doesn't come through every night on schedule."

At that, Mary laughed. "You can get a better view of the train when it goes by if you take your bedroll down by the tracks."

Danny remained resolute. He possessed the wonderful ability to slip seamlessly between his imaginary world and the real one, almost as if the one overlay the other, an ability most children lose with age.

"I don't care what you say. I know the train is coming down the mountain tonight. You just wait and see," he said defensively.

The three prepared their beds in the little tent and turned in. The open end of the tent faced east and overlooked the road. It was a blue-black night with no moon, and the spangled heavens appeared so star-strewn that the major constellations couldn't easily be traced. The tent overlooked the railroad grade much as theater seats overlook a stage, and, indeed, the stage was set. Warm in their bedrolls under the protective canvas, the kids soon dozed off and sleep worked its transformative magic.

In the deep night, Danny bolted upright and woke John and Mary.

"The train just came through! I saw it! Grandpa was the engineer, and he waved at me. Honest!"

"Come on Danny, you're dreaming. Pull the blankets up. It's freezing," John grumped.

Mary echoed John. "Go back to sleep!" she scolded sharply.

Danny lay awake for a time, disturbed by his vision. Had he only been dreaming as John suggested? Or had he really seen the phantom train with Grandpa at the throttle? The remembered image shimmered so vividly that he still trembled. But he couldn't untangle this Gordian knot. Soon the cold and the darkness overcame him, and he, too, fell asleep.

In the morning, after breaking their camp and policing the campsite, the kids climbed into Frances. John cranked the engine over several times until it sputtered, caught, and came to life. Mary and John agreed it had been a great adventure. Danny remained silent, however, seated behind them atop the camping gear. The memory of his vision in the depth of night still disturbed him. He wondered, if it were only a dream, how could it seem so real? Even now, he could clearly see the face of Grandpa Patrick looking directly at him and smiling. He could still hear the squirrel tails of steam hissing from the steam chests, and he could still smell the acrid coal smoke from the locomotive. It simply couldn't have been a dream.

John eased the clutch out and Frances climbed over the grassy berm beside the road. But just as he swung the jeep out onto the old railroad grade, he stepped sharply on the brakes.

"What's wrong?" Mary asked, concern in her voice.

"Nothing's wrong. I just noticed something on the road, and I want to see what it is."

John swung down nimbly from the driver's seat, bowed out of sight, and then climbed back in. Sitting at the steering wheel, he held an object in his hands much as one would hold an open book. He looked down intently at the thing he'd found.

"What is it?" Mary quizzed him impatiently. "Did you find something cool?"

John turned slowly and looked at his brother. "I think it's for you, Danny," John said quietly, handing him a Prince Albert can.

On the ride home, with Frances trundling noisily along Highway 24 across South Park, Danny turned the can over and over in his hands.

"Johnny," he asked, "do you believe me? Or do you think I just dreamed of Grandpa's train?"

John thought for a moment. He didn't want to hurt his brother's feelings. "I don't know, Danny. Lots of pipe smokers drive over the pass, and the can could have been thrown out the window of a car."

Danny's face clouded, and he looked down at the can.

After a couple of minutes, John spoke gently to his brother. "On the other hand, as Shakespeare said, 'There are more things in Heaven and Earth than are dreamt of in your philosophy.'"

Danny looked up puzzled by these elegant words. "What does that mean?"

"It means," answered John, "it *might* have been Grandpa. Who knows?"

Danny's eyes brightened and he smiled. "I *know* it was."

THIRTEEN

THE STRANGE CRITTER OF HOLY CROSS CITY

A hasty glance, and still my heart leaped up,
For still I hoped to see the stranger's *face.*
– Samuel T. Coleridge –

Afternoon sunlight streamed through the window of the class-room where John listened intently to Sister Mary John. She taught him English during his junior and senior years at St. Mary's and had awakened in him a love for poetry. Today, she was explaining the intricacies of the Petrarchan sonnet, and by chance she began analyz-ing Longfellow's touching poem "The Cross of Snow." It immediately captivated John.

"There is a mountain in the distant west,
That sun-defying in its deep ravines,
Displays a cross of snow upon its side."

As she read these metrical lines, the image of the snowy cross glowed in John's imagination. The rest of the poem dealt with love and loss, which made it all the more poignant. When Sister told the students the mountain described in the poem was in Colorado, John became even more intrigued. At supper that evening, he raised the matter with his father.

"Dad," he began, "Do you know where Snowy Cross Mountain is?"

Russell smiled. "You probably mean the Mount of the Holy Cross. It's in the range of peaks south of Minturn. It used to be a national monument until one of the rock ledges supporting the snowy cross broke off. Miners and hunters call that jumble of peaks and forest the Holy Cross country."

Immediately, Danny weighed in. "Can we climb it?"

"Of course, you can climb it, but the hike just to approach the mountain is long and difficult. It's high, stony, and lonesome up there."

John began putting the pieces together. He connected his dad's account with a passage in *Tim Kelley's Fishing Guide to Colorado*. To Colorado fishermen, this book was sacred scripture. The *Guide* described all fishable waters in the state, even some watery rosary of beaver ponds strung along some tiny creek. Most of these places were wild and beautiful. Many were littered with remnants of the state's mining past. One such entry caught John's attention:

> "French Creek flows into Homestake Creek at Gold
> Park after draining Cleveland (French) Lake, Hunky
> Dory Lake, and the Seven Sisters Lakes. An old road
> to Holy Cross City provides access via 4-wheel drive
> as Hunky Dory (11,000 ft; 6 ac) and Cleveland Lake
> (11,920 ft; 20 ac) have brook and cutthroat. Cleveland,
> the better of the two, also has some rainbow."

There it lay, Holy Cross City, smack in the middle of a cluster of remote alpine lakes. John was spellbound. Digging into books and maps, he found that this ghost town began with a modest rush in 1888. It took its name from the Mount of the Holy Cross which rose nearby. A snow-filled crevasse on its face, in the shape of a cross, explained the name of this Fourteener.

In those long-ago days, there were several profitable mines in the Holy Cross district. A stamp mill at Holy Cross City processed the ore from the mines. The concentrates washed down a rickety wooden flume to Gold Park and thence were hauled by wagon to the smelter at Leadville. The boom didn't last long John found out, and by 1910, when the vein in the Pelican Mine played out, the miners abandoned Holy Cross City.

Since then, it languished in decrepit solitude, the buildings going down one by one under the weight of winter snows. As far as John could tell, at the townsite, there yet remained the mill, several buildings, and a number of log foundations. An expedition definitely seemed in order. However, it would have to wait until later in the summer, because the snow would lie deep in the Holy Cross country until July.

On the third Friday of July, having left home in the morning, the kids crossed Tennessee Pass and followed Homestake Creek to Gold Park. Nervous with anticipation, John turned Frances up the trail a later guidebook described as the unholy road leading to Holy Cross City. The trail climbed tortuously for four long miles, with jumbled rock piles, deep mud bogs, stretches of log corduroy, and three creek crossings. The last of these over roaring French Creek was accomplished by creeping carefully across a dilapidated plank bridge.

As Frances crept across that bridge, the planks shifted and groaned ominously. Once past the mill, after clambering up a rock-strewn hill, the jeep rolled into a small meadow littered with the detritus of a bygone world. The kids immediately jumped out and set off to explore Holy Cross City. The remnants of the old town lay all around. The first building they entered was the partially collapsed mill office. Scattered on the floor were invoices and bills, now water-stained and faded. Beneath a desk they found a stack of *National Geographic* magazines from the first decade of the century.

After the mill office, they entered a large log building that doubtless served both as a dwelling and a stable. Several rope bridles hung on the wall, with old pieces of harness leather scattered across the floor. Next on their tour came the store. The entry door opened into a small room with a counter and shelves on the walls. In the back room, probably used for storage, the kids found an interesting graffito. Written in a strong hand on the planed surface of one of the walls, the inscription said "Lingo the Drifter, And Yaller Hair, Novice, 1957."

"Who do you think he was?" Mary asked.

"I bet he was a bandit or a desperado," offered Danny.

John laughed. "What's the difference, Danny?"

"Well, I think desperadoes kill people, and bandits just rob them." Danny emphasized *kill* strongly lending authority to his distinction.

Fifty years later, on a whimsical internet search, Mary discovered that Lingo was a folk singer, hardly a desperado, who came west to Colorado from Chicago in 1955. Apparently, he also visited Holy Cross City in the summer of 1957. Lingo enjoyed a modest musical career and then settled into a home in the hills west of Denver, becoming a new age guru to a generation of Denver flower children. The old store at Holy Cross City would be known to the Grays thereafter as Lingo's cabin.

Across the main street from the store, the foundation of a saloon stood about three logs high. Handblown bottles of various sizes and colors festooned the grassy space that had once been the dance floor. John found an old hat under a pile of boards, which he proudly donned after a vigorous shaking. He would wear this hat for several years thereafter until it succumbed to age.

"How do I look?" he asked his brother and sister.

"You look like a desperado," Mary quipped.

Only one building remained to be toured. It was a small frame structure sheathed with vertical planks, not fitted logs like the other buildings, and obviously of more recent vintage. Perhaps it was a line shack used by sheep herders or cowboys when they grazed livestock in this high country. Its furnishings included a potbelly stove, a table, and triple bunks, with two shuttered windows and a working door. After a cursory inspection, all three agreed this should be headquarters for their two-day visit. John then trotted the several hundred yards back

Golden Mantled Ground Squirrel
Spermophilus lateralis

Mary's Quarry

to the jeep, and having fired Frances up again, guided her through the maze of log foundations and parked her beside the shack.

That evening, after a fine supper of fried potatoes, beans, and sausage prepared on the stove, the three made their beds on the wood slat bunks. All went well for several hours, but later in the night, the pack rats that lived beneath the shack invaded the room. They raced back and forth, rattled pans, scampered across the kids' faces, and in general made themselves a nuisance.

Dawn came cold and clear, and when the rats retreated, the kids got a couple of hours of uninterrupted sleep. Upon rising, however, they agreed: despite the comforts of the shack, the next night they'd sleep outside in their pup tent.

Saturday morning was glorious and rich with promise. From among the many tantalizing choices, the kids followed their interests. Mary set out to trap a ground squirrel. Her trap consisted of a small cardboard box propped up with a stick, with an apple wedge for bait. Once she'd successfully trapped her quarry, a certainty in her mind, she would turn to photographing wildflowers that flourished in lush profusion all over the meadow. John and Danny intended to fish for a few hours in the Mulhall Lakes, and, after they returned to camp, the three would explore the many ruins in the townsite and surrounding forest.

At the lakes, the boys had a grand experience. The upper lake yielded countless small brook trout. At the lower lake which contained larger fish, the two boys practiced what they called "hunt fishing." John taught Danny, patiently coaching his brother. This technique involved watching for trout cruising along the shore of the lake.

"Look straight out, Danny! There's a beaut! Do you see him?"

"Oh, yeah! He *is* a beaut!" Danny responded excitedly.

"Now, make a couple of false casts to get your line out, and drop your fly about five feet in front of him," John instructed.

Danny stripped out some line, keeping it in the air, and then made a fine cast just where John had advised. The twelve-inch brookie shot up, seized the royal coachman, and dove into the darker, deeper water. Danny patiently pulled the fish in, and after the two brothers briefly admired its brilliant colors, Danny gently released it back into the lake.

"That was great, Danny! You're becoming a fine fisherman. Not as good as I, but fine nevertheless."

The fishing thrill of the afternoon came when the boys set off for their camp. The trail passed a very small tarn that lay on the outlet creek from Upper Mulhall Lake. This little pothole hardly deserved the term lake. It was just a snow water pond, so shallow they could see the bottom easily all the way across, except for the deep blue streak down the middle that marked the stream channel. John knew such tarns were typically sterile, but if there were a deep channel, it could harbor a few trout that might have washed down as fry from the lake above. More out of curiosity than anything, John threw his fly, quartering upstream, onto the deep channel. The red variant floated jauntily down the current until directly abreast of the boys.

Suddenly, like a stalking submarine, a large form emerged out of the opaque depths of the channel, vectoring in on John's red variant. The fish struck savagely. John set the hook, and eventually played the fish out and reeled it in. The fish amazed Danny, surely the largest trout he'd ever seen in the wild. The big brookie measured eighteen inches and went to several pounds. The boys admired it briefly, and then John eased it into the water, moving it back and forth to circulate water through its gills. When the fish began squirming, he released it back into the pond, whereupon it shot out of sight into the dark channel. Danny would remember this vignette all his life – his brother John, master of anglers, the gorgeous trout, the sunny afternoon, all in this wild country.

As the boys came down the rutted road into the town, Mary shouted happily, "I caught a squirrel!"

The kids found a piece of window screen next to the shack which John slipped between the box and the trapped squirrel. Taking care, they turned the trap over. The squirrel caromed from edge to edge in the box, but settled down and seemed to accept its captivity.

"We'll keep him as our mascot until we leave tomorrow," said John. "Then we'll have to turn him loose."

Mary agreed reluctantly. "All right, but he'll be fun to watch until we leave." In her heart she knew this ground squirrel wouldn't survive once taken out of its mountain home.

For the next hour, the kids explored the thick spruce forest around the old town. There were countless remnants of the mining days scattered around. They found rotted rubber hoses, rusty iron pipes, and a one-cylinder diesel engine – all the things that were the warp and woof of late nineteenth century mining life. There were also many foundations and old cabins moldering into the mossy ground.

At one such cabin, Mary made an exciting discovery. Under a large flat rock nearby, she saw what seemed to be a leather bag. Just the corner of the bag protruded, with a brass buckle and leather strap. The rock weighed too much for the kids, and, using a stick, Mary could only scratch around in the stony soil. John took over the excavation job, but could do no better. When he pulled on the strap, the rotten leather broke off. At this point, they decided it must be a pair of saddle bags.

This discovery puzzled them. Someone obviously buried the bags to retrieve them later. The bank-leery miners commonly stashed gold in such places. The three eventually gave up in frustration. They vowed to bring proper digging tools the next time they came in order to unearth this treasure. And so they did, returning several times over the years as adults, always trying to find the buried saddle bags. But landscape is alive and changes dramatically over time. Despite their best efforts, they could never relocate the site of the buried treasure. After the last such failed attempt, thirty years later, John pronounced the saddle bag treasure officially lost, and it entered into family lore.

John and Danny pitched the pup tent before dinner and moved their bed rolls out of the shack. The three were determined to avoid the pack rats during the coming night. However, the cozy shack, warmed by the glowing stove and lighted with John's sputtering white-gas lantern, was perfect for their supper and late evening storytelling. Mary sliced thick slabs from a Danish canned ham as a special treat. They prepared a savory meal of ham, baked potatoes, and beans. The meals on their expeditions tended to be repetitive, but in the kids' view, it would be hard to improve on them.

After supper cleanup, and with all the stove wood burned, the three retired to the tent. The night was moonless, and though millions of stars shone from the dome of heaven, an inky blackness enveloped the meadow. Sleep settled swiftly upon them.

Danny awoke in the deep night, startled and frightened. Someone or something was groping him through the tent wall. Strong hands were slowly moving over his body, as if trying to discern what lay within the tent. It took Danny several seconds to clear his mind and to respond to this terrifying experience.

"Johnny and Mary!" he yelled. "Somebody's grabbing me through the tent wall!"

At the sound of his voice, the hands immediately ceased their exploration. Danny trembled now from shock and fear.

John's initial inclination was to chide Danny for waking them up. Wasn't this just like the ghost train at Marshall Pass? Instead, he tried to calm him. "It's all right, Danny. You must've had a nightmare."

"No, I didn't!" Danny insisted. "Something grabbed me!"

John picked up the flashlight beside his bed and shone it around inside the tent and out the opening at the front. Nothing. Then, he went outside into the black night, slowly sweeping the light across the meadow toward the dense wall of timber thirty yards away. Nothing. By now, Mary and Danny had joined him, and what they saw next stunned them. A heavy dew fell that night, and the cold had glazed the meadow grass with frost. The mysterious visitor had trampled down the frost, leaving a clearly visible trackway circling the tent. No one in the tent slept for the rest of the night.

At dawn, they found another strange sign. They'd eaten only half the canned ham for supper the previous evening, and saved the remaining half still in the can for breakfast. Before they bedded down, they'd placed it on a high shelf on the outside wall of the shack. In the morning, to their amazement, the can still sat on the shelf, but the ham had vanished. There were no remnants as if the ham had been gnawed by small animals. The ham had been cleanly removed from the can.

"John, what stalked us last night," asked Mary, "maybe some crazy man or an escaped convict from the Cañon City prison?"

"I have no idea. I will say this: it was a strange critter," John replied.

"That's it! It was *the* Strange Critter!" Danny enthused, his fear having subsided now that they were out in broad daylight.

There in the heart of the Holy Cross country, with hundreds of thousands of acres of dark timber, deep canyons, and alpine tundra, the three Gray kids sat bemused on a sunlit rock and talked about the events of the night. In this vast wilderness, all things were possible. After a while, with a mixture of emotions – joy, anxiety, curiosity, wonder – they loaded their camp into Frances, and began the four-mile descent of the Holy Cross City trail to Gold Park and the road home. Later, rolling along the Arkansas River below Leadville, John and Mary discussed at length their experience. Danny kept a meditative silence.

At length, he said, "Johnny, remember what you told me about there being many things in Heaven and Earth we don't understand? I think this is one of them."

In January, 1968, when Helen and Dan honeymooned in Colorado Springs, they passed an afternoon browsing in the Chinook Bookstore. Helen saw an interesting title, and pulled it down from the shelf. The book contained stories of the mining days in Colorado. One chapter in the table of contents immediately arrested her gaze. It read: "The Abominable Snowman of Half-Moon Gulch." The story cited an article in the *Leadville Chronicle* from the 1880s in which two miners, upon returning to their cabin in Half-Moon Gulch, surprised two tall, hairy, ape-like creatures. Excited, she brought the cryptic reference to Dan's attention. The bookstore had a stock of USGS quadrangle maps, and when they found the map showing Holy Cross City, they saw that Half-Moon Gulch lay only a couple of miles, as the crow flies, from the ghost town. Here, indeed, was their *Strange Critter*!

For many years and even cycles of years, around summer campfires, two generations of the Gray family have enjoyed the story of "The Strange Critter of Holy Cross City." This mysterious tale, now burnished to brightness through countless retellings, has become the epicenter of family lore, "changeless," as Longfellow said, "through all the changing scenes and seasons."

FOURTEEN

FAREWELL TO COLORADO

i thank You God for most this amazing
day: for the leaping greenly spirit of trees
and a blue true dream of sky; and for everything
which is natural which is infinite which is yes
— e. e. cummings —

Several weeks after their Holy Cross City adventure, just before the beginning of school, John sat at the Gray supper table, lost in his thoughts. He harbored misgivings about going to college in distant San Francisco. He hadn't even left yet, and he was already homesick.

What seemed so romantic and exciting six months ago now began to lose its luster. His departure for college might be viewed as a beginning, but closeness to family and love for his native haunts made leaving a daunting thing. In his heart he knew a special time was drawing to a close. He knew he would come home from time to time, but he also knew that his life would never again be the same. These last two years were like a dream for him, all joy and wonder and happiness. What the future held was uncertain. He didn't really fear these changes, but leaving what he knew and loved made him inexpressibly sad. He longed to do something with his family, something that would coin a memory to cherish when he lived far away.

"I have an idea for this coming Sunday. Let's all go for a picnic up to Rule Creek. Mom and Dad, we can show you where we camped last summer and where Fred is living. I'm leaving for college in a week, and Danny will be entering high school. It would be a celebration of the end of a great summer and the beginning of new chapters in our lives."

"How would we get there?" asked Louise.

"John can take all of us in Frances," Danny piped up. "John and Dad can ride in the front seats. Mom, you and Mary can ride in back, and I'll ride between the front seats on a pillow. We can pack the food behind the back seat. We could also stash our fly rods just in case there is a good hatch going on."

"It would be a bucket of laughs, but I think we can do it," offered Russell, who'd been quiet up to this point.

Louise spoke up, settling the matter. "A family picnic would be fun, and I'd love to see Rule Creek. I say let's go!"

⸻

Sunday dawned bright and beautiful, with a blue sky and a few clouds scudding over the mountains. The Grays were packed and on the road by ten in the morning. With Louise running the show, everything went like clockwork. The family and their picnic filled Frances jam-full, but the seating arrangements worked fine, with everyone in high spirits. During the long haul up Ute Pass, the kids told over again the stories of their adventures last August and November. Before they knew it, there stood the rusty coffee can where they turned onto the secret road.

Mary recreated the struggle at the big snow drift. Her natural gift for drama made the story exciting. Just as if planned, when she described how they finally burst out of the snow, she made a grand flourish with her hand and pointed to the rocks and sticks that still littered the trail.

"You kids were lucky. It would have been a long, cold walk to Divide," Russell scolded them gently. "Don't forget that lesson."

"Aw, Dad, I never doubted for a moment we could make it out. We just had to be resourceful," responded John.

"Yeah, Dad, we were *resourceful*!" seconded Danny, taking pleasure in such a fine word.

Hermit Thrush
Catharus guttatus

Rosy Paintbrush
Castilleja rhexifolia

Columbine
Aquilegia caerules

Hermit Thrush and Wildflowers

One last turn of the trail and they rolled out into the Rule Creek meadow. How different it looked from the wintry place when last visited. The aspens were in leaf, their leaves clicking musically in the light breeze. The beaver ponds were full, with water cascading over the dams. Rule Creek remained exactly the paradise they remembered.

"This valley is lovely," said Louise. "It's the perfect picnic place."

When they came to the big pond, John stopped the jeep and turned off the engine. This seemed like an ideal spot. They could have their picnic on the grass right next to the pond.

"Come on, Mom and Dad. I want to show you where we camped," said Mary.

She walked backwards in front of her parents like a tour guide gesturing and explaining, showing them where they'd pitched their tent and where their fire ring had been. Then she led them into the aspen glade so they could see the variety and beauty of the wildflowers she'd photographed.

When they returned, John and Danny took over and pointed out to Russell exactly where they stood while fishing and talked excitedly about the mayfly hatch and how frantic the fishing had been. Russell didn't doubt their story. Even as the boys gave their animated account, the pond sparkled with the rings of rising trout. After they'd eaten, Russell suggested perhaps they could wet a line.

Louise had made an elaborate picnic lunch with all the things the kids loved. It included abundant ham and cheese sandwiches, potato salad, corn chips, green olives, and Rice Crispy treats for dessert. They brought this traditional picnic lunch because the kids always insisted on exactly the same fare. Having spread out the blankets that had served as Danny's seat, everyone enjoyed the meal prepared by Louise. Suddenly, Russell pointed to the shallow water only a couple of feet in front of them.

"Look! There are some little trout!"

In the water next to the bank, trout fingerlings darted this way and that chasing mosquito larvae.

"They're rainbows." he said.

"How can you tell, Dad," asked Danny.

"If they were brookies, they'd have white fin edges."

"Maybe they're Fred's babies," Danny enthused. "They *could* be, you know. He could be a dad."

"I have no doubt," Louise said, laughing at the charming idea of Fred the Trout having offspring.

For a while, the family lounged on the grassy banks of the beaver pond enjoying the serenity of this beautiful place. Then, Danny did something quite unexpected. He picked up a leftover bread crust, rolled it between his fingers into a little ball, and threw it. The ball arced through the air and landed twenty feet out in the pond. Immediately, a beautiful twelve-inch rainbow slashed through the surface of the pond and pounced on the bread.

"I bet that's Fred!" Danny said excitedly.

Russell smiled at his younger son. "You know, Danny, it doesn't really matter whether that particular fish is Fred or not. It doesn't change what you did last winter when you brought him here. That was a good thing, and I was proud of you for trying to save Fred's life. In the end, life is about stringing together good things until they gather to a greatness. It isn't the things themselves that matter, but that you try to bring them about."

Danny knew trout were in these mountain creeks since the last Ice Age. Fred had become a part of the great story, the long, manifold saga of life. Danny's heart swelled. By saving Fred and bringing him here, he, too, played a part in the story of the world, if only a small part. He'd done a grown-up thing, though, and he was proud. Of course, no one could tell if the leaping rainbow were Fred. But, in Danny's heart there remained no doubt. It *was* Fred.

<hr>

That emblematic moment at the end of such a fine day seemed almost too good, too enjoyable to be true. But, as Heraclitus said long ago, "All things change, nothing abides." Over the ridge to the west came a churning mass of clouds, dark and ominous. This storm hadn't been predicted in the morning forecast. Now, it threatened to engulf the valley, with lightning forking and dancing in front of the black wall of thunderheads.

All the Grays sensed the danger and frantically gathered up the remains of their picnic. The table cloth became a large bag as Russell pulled the four corners together, hobo style, and stuffed this big sack into the rear of the jeep. In no time at all, they were fleeing up the rocky trail out of the valley. In a few minutes, the rain came with lightning crackling all around. Russell realized they couldn't outrun the storm.

"John, do you see that big ponderosa on the left side of the road? Work Frances in as closely as you can to the trunk."

The tree stood massive and tall with a spreading crown. The lower ten feet of its huge trunk were free of branches allowing the jeep to snuggle in tightly. No sooner had John switched off the engine than the hail began. At first, the hailstones were dime-size, and they beat a desultory tattoo on the ground and the trees. The crown of the big ponderosa was so dense that, like a great umbrella, none were able to strike the jeep. But, when the full force of the storm came, jagged clumps of ice as large as baseballs came plunging out of the windblown rain with terrifying fury. Limbs crashed down from the top of the tree. Five or six inches of hail quickly covered everything, transforming a pristine summer day into a bizarre wintry landscape. Inside Frances everyone was mute, stunned into silence by the fury of the storm. It had become a maelstrom of howling wind, lightning, and hail as if the end of the world were at hand. Then, just as suddenly as it came, the storm passed.

John looked at his father. "Wow!"

From his perch between the two front seats, Danny echoed that sentiment, "Wow!"

Everyone burst into animated speech, gesturing, laughing, holding hands, and hugging. Not only had they witnessed a great storm, but, intuitively, they realized they'd survived something dark and predatory.

John fired up Frances and got underway. They crept forward slowly, with the wary caution of infantrymen rising out of their foxholes after a great battle. The going became very difficult, since the large hail formed icy ball bearings that made the jeep slew almost uncontrollably as it climbed the remaining half mile out of the valley. When they turned onto the gravel county road, the magnitude of the event they'd just witnessed struck them with full force.

On the ridgetop was a grassy meadow adjacent to the road in which a local rancher pastured a few cattle. All of them lay on the ground, scattered about the meadow, beaten to death by the huge hail stones, several still convulsing in their death agony. John stopped the jeep beside the fence; all the Grays stared at the carnage in disbelief.

"Russ," Louise said with measured care, "that tree saved us. If we hadn't sheltered under it, the hail would've shredded the jeep's canvas top instantly, and the storm would've killed us as surely as it killed the cows."

The mood in Frances was subdued, and the ride back to Colorado Springs passed in relative silence. The truth of Cicero's dictum, *Signa rerum futurarum a dis ostenduntur*, was about to be impressed upon the Gray family. Indeed, signs of future things are revealed by the gods.

On a morning several days after the Rule Creek picnic, Louise sat opposite Russell in the breakfast nook in the Gray kitchen. With her face buried in her hands, she sobbed inconsolably.

Russell, beside himself, sat silently with his eyes closed. How could he soothe her unhappiness, how would he explain to the kids the blow that had befallen him that morning? For no evident reason, and without explanation, his landlord refused to renew the lease on the building housing the Green Pine Restaurant. Everything in their lives would now be turned topsy-turvy. Russell would have to find another job. He'd made his living at the Green Pine since John's infancy. The chances of finding comparable work in Colorado Springs, a small town with limited economic opportunities, were slim. The Grays would probably have to move. This would mean John's college plans would have to be deferred. Mary and Danny would have to change schools, one of the worst conceivable disasters in the mind of a child.

Louise and Russell were entering middle age. They'd lived through the Great Depression and survived the war, and were just beginning to enjoy a stable and prosperous life. Until today, they'd looked forward to the coming years, assured about their economic situation, pleased with the way their kids were turning out, settled and content.

Only a few days before, their lives had been idyllic. They'd celebrated the congenial warmth of their love for one another at the Rule Creek picnic. Sitting on the grassy banks of the beaver pond talking and laughing together, none of the Grays could have imagined the staggering changes the following days would bring, days of uncertainty, struggle, anger, and failed hopes.

When Russell told the kids about the loss of the restaurant, there were tears all around. His demeanor remained laconic, but Louise's family had what the Irish called "the gift of tears," and she'd passed that on to her kids. At first, the kids were incredulous. How could this be? Couldn't this situation be managed? Couldn't Mr. Kurtz be persuaded to reconsider?

Russell responded to each of these hopeful questions, a task almost too painful to bear. No, things couldn't be changed. He saw no way to give their old lives back to them.

———◆———

A funereal mood hung over the Gray home for the next several weeks. Russell drove to Phoenix where a business acquaintance had arranged an interview for him. Louise supervised the painful process of uprooting her children from their lives on Elm Circle. Fortunately, Russell quickly landed a job managing a hotel in Phoenix. He purchased a small tract house in a new subdivision on the eastern edge of the city. It was a far cry from Elm Circle, no view of snow-capped Pikes Peak, no prairie vista, no woods, no pond, nothing spacious, nothing gracious, but it would do. Calling Louise long distance from Phoenix, he assured her in his inimitable way that they'd be fine. Russell returned briefly to finalize all the departure arrangements: a mover to be hired, the house to be listed for sale, and myriad annoying but essential loose ends to tie up.

Finally, their friends threw a going away party with tearful farewells from all. Everyone said how wretched their fate was, all voiced outrage at the mindless cruelty of business as usual. Finally, the friends left, group by group, with handshakes and kisses and promises of visits. The Grays – Louise and Russell, John, Mary, and Danny – retired to their bedrooms after which Louise switched off the lights of their beloved Elm Circle home for the last time.

EPILOGUE

Backward, flow backward, O tide of the years!
I am so weary of toil and of tears, –
Toil without recompense, Tears all in vain, –
Take them and give me my childhood again!
– Elizabeth A. Allen –

In July, 2011, Dan Gray attended the fiftieth anniversary reunion of the senior class of 1961. This was the first reunion since they'd left St. Mary's High School. Dan went to school with these fifty men and women from kindergarten through eighth grade, but his family moved away in the autumn of 1957, and, as a consequence, he hadn't gone to high school with them. Nonetheless, they considered him to be a member of their class, and it pleased him to be invited. Somehow, a reunion never seemed an important thing to these folks, but after the passage of fifty years – college, marriages, children, careers, and retirement – his classmates thought it would be good to gather once again.

It was the first time he'd seen any of them since the Gray family left Colorado Springs. The experience was poignant and bittersweet. It shocked him to see his little band of friends now turned into old men and women. In his mind's eye, the images of Frank, Ted, Tom, and Larry as mischievous, twelve-year-old rascals continually intruded upon and overlay his current perceptions of them as affable old men, happily regaling one another, catching up on decades of separated lives. The girls as well, winsome and fetching long ago, had become matronly and loquacious. On a purely conceptual level, he knew he'd aged similarly. But, since he saw himself every day, he wasn't always mindful of the relentless assault of time.

Happiness abounded in old friendships renewed, but also sadness, as several from the class were deceased. Again, although he knew these deaths had occurred, the actual realization of absence touched him. He remembered Mary Jo. She'd been his sweetheart in kindergarten, and she remained so all through grade school. He remembered her at their eighth-grade graduation dance, blue-eyed and blonde, radiating effervescent joy. To her delight, he'd written his name on every line of her dance card. There were several others, as well, who peopled the memories of his boyhood.

After two days of talking, laughing, and crying, the class attended a concluding afternoon picnic at Austin Bluffs. Once they finished the meal and final goodbyes were said, the old classmates departed, all to their real lives, leaving behind this brief reliving of their shared golden age. There were promises all around about another reunion in five years. Dan hoped it would be so.

That evening in his hotel room, he called his son, Paul, who lived in Durango.

"Son, could you get a couple of days off? I thought we might do something before I head back to St. Louis."

"Sure, Dad, no problem. What do you have in mind?"

"It would be really fine to hike up to Holy Cross City. We could hang out in Lingo's cabin and pester the brookies in the Mulhall Lakes. If you could meet me tomorrow afternoon at the trailhead around five, we might make it to the City before dark. I'll stop at the Safeway in Leadville and buy food."

Dan brought his backpack and the requisite gear to the reunion on the off chance he might be able to go to the mountains. It pleased Dan that his son could join him. Over the years, Holy Cross City

Lingo's Cabin, Holy Cross City Townsite

had become a kind of pilgrimage site for the Grays. On the wall of Lingo's cabin, there's a graffito that lists the years of their visits, going back to the first trip taken by the three kids back in 1957. Someone in the family had gone up to the ghost town in almost all of the intervening years.

⊸•⊸

As is usually the case, both Paul and he were waylaid by events, and both arrived at the trailhead at about the same time, but several hours late. The sunny afternoon had given way to a cloudy sky, with occasional light rain. After dark, a misty fog diffused through the utterly still air. It was a beautiful evening, with a full moon glowing dimly through the clouds. Both men shouldered their packs and started up the jeep road, chatting happily and picking their way over the rocky trail by the light of their headlamps.

They reached the site of the ghost town about ten, and, planning to sleep in Lingo's cabin, were pleased to find it dark and empty. The two men didn't see any signs of recent travelers on the road, and now they found the meadow and the old town altogether deserted. The cabin roof was gradually failing and the front part no longer protected against rain. However, the makeshift stove and the back half of the cabin were still covered and dry.

Dan and Paul leaned their packs against the back wall just under the cryptic scribble of Lingo the Drifter. After inflating their sleeping pads, they laid them on the floor in the back corner of the room and rolled out their sleeping bags.

Previous visitors had thoughtfully left a stack of firewood beside the stove, so supper could be easily gotten up. Dan brought along two steaks, two potatoes, a can of baked beans, and a six-pack of beer. Once the fire burned down to coals, they baked the potatoes, heated the beans, and broiled the steaks. The two men savored this delicious fare, made doubly enjoyable by their conversation. The Grays were inveterate backpackers, and in their particular style of trail life, supper and conversation around the night fire were the zenith of any day in the mountains.

With the beer mostly gone and the firewood mostly burned, the two men turned in. By now the sky had cleared, and the full moon shone. The chinking between many of the logs in the cabin walls was gone, and shafts of moonlight streamed into the room.

"What an awesome walk tonight, Dad," Paul remarked. "I've hiked that road many times, and this was the best. I loved the mysterious atmosphere, walking in the mist. I felt as if I were walking into my own past."

I agree," seconded Dan. "I had this sense that Mom walked with us, my brother and sister, and the spirits of Grandma and Grandpa as well. Isn't it wonderful how those whom you love are always somehow with you? They *were* walking with us tonight. Let the materialists say what they will; there *are* more things in Heaven and on Earth than are dreamt of in their philosophy."

"You're right, Dad. Your family is connected to you even when you're unaware of them. Many times over the years, I've been startled by you speaking to me, speaking so clearly I even noted the tone of your voice."

"I know, Son. My dad had a very distinctive footfall. I remember hearing him walking up the aisle of St. Mary's, taking up the collection at Mass on Sunday. Without looking over my shoulder, I could tell by the sound of his steps it was he coming up the aisle. At various times in my life I've heard his footfalls. On a number of occasions, as well, I have clearly heard my mother call 'Danny!' It's quite mysterious."

After a moment, Paul responded. "You know, Dad, Molly's request that you write down the memories of your boyhood was foreseeing. Those stories have made our family's past so present. Though we've all pursued separate lives, in a wonderful way your stories help us to live together still."

Though tired, both men were happy. Their talk continued in this vein until it gradually faded and sleep overcame them.

In the morning, after breakfast of bacon and eggs, they took their coffee outside the cabin and sat down on a flat granite boulder near the door, the same boulder on which Dan sat with John and Mary so long ago. To the east spread a panorama of lesser peaks rising up to and falling away from Homestake Peak. In the far distance, they could see the ragged skyline of the Ten Mile Range and the Mosquito Range. To the north towered the granite mass of Whitney Peak. To the west loomed Critter Mountain, named by the Gray kids many years ago, because they imagined their Strange Critter lived in a hidden lair on its summit. Two small creeks coursed through the meadow which made the townsite a natural arboretum. Near at hand, and all around, wildflowers bloomed.

Paul reached down and plucked a single blossom from a clump of columbine growing at the base of their boulder. Cupping it in his hand, he began speaking:

> "Flower in the crannied wall,
> I pluck you out of the crannies,
> I hold you here, root and all, in my hand
> Little flower – but if I could understand
> What you are, root and all, all in all,
> I should know what God and man is."

Handing the blossom to his dad, he said, "When all the talk about poetry and beautiful language is over, this is my favorite piece. In it, Tennyson says everything worth saying."

"I love it as well," replied Dan, "That's why I taught it to you years ago."

Father and his son sat quietly in the warm sun. Finally, Dan said, "The simplest things are often best. You know how lines from a poem or a song will stick in your mind and become a permanent part of your mental furniture? There's a verse from a Christmas carol I've always loved."

Dan began humming, then sang softly:

> "I love thee, Lord Jesus, look down from the sky,
> And stay by my cradle till morning is nigh."

He paused thoughtfully, remembering a similar conversation with his brother, John, many years before.

"Aside from the religious sentiment, the idea these lines express is so hopeful. No matter how difficult or bleak life becomes, ultimately, God's will for mankind is that we be happy. Whatever befalls us, Providence will show a path. I realize 'the world is full of sorrow, and hearts must break and bleed,' but much of that is because we're free and often bring disaster upon ourselves."

"True. But here's where it gets complicated, Dad. The moral excellence of a person doesn't seem to matter. There's no logic for either our prosperity or our suffering. As Hopkins says,

> 'Oh, the sots and thralls of lust
> Do in spare hours more thrive than I that spend,
> Sir, life upon thy cause.'"

"I know, I know," Dan responded. "I wrestle with this paradox all the time. In my mind, it's the central problem of human existence. No answer is completely satisfying, and it ends up being a matter of trust. If we could understand the order of the universe brought about by God's love, we would see that it exceeds all our hopes though its goodness often seems elusive. Even when the night is very dark, we have to believe the Earth will spin one more time and dawn will sweep over us again, *because morning is always nigh.*

Paul stood up and stretched. Then he bent down and squeezed his father's shoulder gently. "Come on, Dad. Let's go fishing."

LINGO'S CABIN

"Lingo the Drifter and Yaller Hair"
Graffito in a ghost town cabin

His name became an emblem for my fears,
This man I never knew whose penciled scrawl
Had left a statement there upon a wall
Of rough-sawn boards. So, through the mazy years
I drift, and find no power with which to write
My name, to state outright that this is I,
This deed I've done, this much I've been. I sigh
As afternoon for me moves on to night.
Perhaps that's all there is to being a man,
To write one's name upon a weathered wall,
And go, like a spark the chilling wind might fan
From the campfire into the starry night where all
Things go at last. Perhaps there is no plan,
But just the common dark where coyotes call.

–John Wickersham–

LIST OF QUOTATIONS AND ALLUSIONS

1. Alfred Tennyson, "Tears, Idle Tears"
2. William C. Bryant, "Thanatopsis"
3. Robert Browning, "Pippa Passes"
4. William B. Yeats, "Song of Wandering Aengus"
5. Horace, *Odes, III, 13*
6. John Wickersham, "Old Jeeps"
7. John Magee, "High Flight"
8. Patricia Bunn, "Gang Poetry"
9. Gerard M. Hopkins, "Pied Beauty"
10. Robert Herrick, "To the Virgins, to Make Much of Time"
11. William B. Yeats, "The Lake Isle of Innisfree"
12. "Cielito Lindo," Mexican Folk Song
13. Maxwell Anderson, "September Song"
14. Percy B. Shelley, "Ode to the West Wind"
15. Robert M. Crawford, "The U.S. Air Force Song"
16. Thomas Aquinas, *Summa of Theology*
17. William W. Longfellow, "Snow-Flakes"
18. John Wickersham, "The Snowfall"
19. Terry Gilkyson, "Cry of the Wild Goose"
20. William C. Bryant, "To a Waterfowl"
21. Phillip Bliss, "Dare to Be a Daniel"
22. Aldo Leopold, *Sand County Almanac*
23. M. E. Abbey, "Life Is Like a Mountain Railroad"
24. William Shakespeare, "Hamlet"
25. Samuel T. Coleridge, "Frost at Midnight"
26. William W. Longfellow, "The Cross of Snow"
27. e. e. cummings, "i thank You God for most this amazing"
28. Heraclitus, *The Fragments of Heraclitus*
29. Cicero, *On the Nature of the Gods*
30. Elizabeth A. Allen, "Rock Me to Sleep"
31. Alfred Tennyson, "Flower in the Crannied Wall"
32. Charles H. Gabriel, "Away in a Manger"
33. Gerard M. Hopkins, 'Thou are indeed just, Lord, if I contend'
34. Cy Warman, "Creede"

THE *SERIOUS ABOUT WRITING* PUBLISHING PACKAGE

Are you interested in publishing your fiction or non-fiction title with the prestige of an imprint? Do you want a staff of editors and designers to provide the best quality product possible? Is it important to keep your copyright and all profits from your book sales? Oh, and would you like it done in three months instead of the typical 18 months to two years required by a traditional publisher?

Look into our *Serious About Writing* package. We don't take commissions and don't give advances. We review your manuscript regardless if it's sent by you or by an agent. In exchange for an up-front one-time fee, we make sure your work is in the best shape possible and receives the acceptance it deserves.

Here are just some of the advantages:
- Expert editing and design staff.
- Personal service throughout all aspects of the process.
- Prestige of a third-party publisher.
- Distribution to Amazon, Kindle, and other outlets.
- Creation of ISBN & bar code.
- Retention of all copyrights.
- One hundred percent royalties.
- Completion and publication within 90 days.
- A marketing plan that can be implemented by the author.

You can choose multiple avenues to accomplish these same tasks, or take advantage of the *Serious About Writing* package. Contact us for more information at woodenpantspub@gmail.com. You can also visit our website, woodenpantspub.com, and fill out the form on the Publication page. We look forward to working with you toward your goal of author entrepreneurship!